咆哮山莊

Wuthering Heights

原著 _ Emily Brontë

改寫 _ Jennifer Gascoigne

譯者 _ 安卡斯

國家圖書館出版品預行編目資料

咆哮山莊 / Emily Brontë 著；安卡斯 譯. —初版. —[臺北市] : 寂天文化, 2013.10　面；公分.

中英對照

ISBN 978-986-318-158-3 (25K平裝附光碟片)

1.英語 2.讀本

805.18　　　　　　　　　102019592

原著 _ Emily Brontë
改寫 _ Jennifer Gascoigne
譯者 _ 安卡斯
校對 _ 陳慧莉
製程管理 _ 宋建文
出版者 _ 寂天文化事業股份有限公司
電話 _ +886-2-2365-9739
傳真 _ +886-2-2365-9835
網址 _ www.icosmos.com.tw
讀者服務 _ onlineservice@icosmos.com.tw
出版日期 _ 2013年10月 初版一刷（250101）

郵撥帳號 _
1998620-0 寂天文化事業股份有限公司

ABOUT THIS BOOK

For the Student

🎧 Listen to the story and do some activities on your Audio CD.

💬 Talk about the story.

⭐ Prepare for Cambridge English: Preliminary (PET) for schools

For the Teacher

HELBLING e·ZONE THE EDUCATIONAL PLATFORM A state-of-the-art interactive learning environment with 1000s of free online self-correcting activities for your chosen readers.

Go to our Readers Resource site for information on using readers and downloadable Resource Sheets, photocopiable Worksheets, and Tapescripts. www.helblingreaders.com

For lots of great ideas on using Graded Readers consult Reading Matters, the Teacher's Guide to using Helbling Readers.

Level 4 Structures

Sequencing of future tenses	Could / was able to / managed to
Present perfect plus yet, already, just	Had to / didn't have to
First conditional	Shall / could for offers
Present and past passive	May / can / could for permission Might for future possibility
How long?	Make and let
Very / really / quite	Causative have Want / ask / tell someone to do something

Structures from lower levels are also included.

CONTENTS

ABOUT THE AUTHOR

Emily Brontë was born on July 30th, 1818, the fifth child of six. When she was three years old, her mother died and the children were brought up[1] by an aunt. They lived in the parsonage[2] in Haworth, a village in West Yorkshire, because their father was the parson[3] there. The village was on the edge[4] of a large moor[5] and this landscape was the inspiration[6] for Emily's writing.

For a short time she attended[7] a school with her older sisters Maria, Elizabeth and Charlotte. When Maria and Elizabeth both died of tuberculosis[8] in 1825, Charlotte and Emily were taken home. After that they were educated with their brother Branwell by their father at the parsonage.

Emily loved the beautiful, windswept[9] Yorkshire countryside around Haworth and became sad and ill when she was away from it. She had a job as a private[10] teacher for a short time in 1837, and in 1842 she went to Belgium with Charlotte to study French and German at a girls' academy[11]. Later the two sisters opened a school in their own home but they had to close it because they didn't have enough students. Haworth was too far from big towns and cities for most people.

Emily, Charlotte and their younger sister Anne all enjoyed writing. In 1846 they published[12] a collection of their poetry[13]. The following year Emily's only novel *Wuthering[14] Heights[15]* was published. Emily Brontë died of tuberculosis in December 1848 and is buried in Haworth.

1 bring up 養育長大
2 parsonage [ˈpɑrsṇɪdʒ] (n.) 牧師公館
3 parson [ˈpɑrsṇ] (n.) 教區牧師
4 edge [ɛdʒ] (n.) 邊緣
5 moor [mʊr] (n.) 荒野；曠野
6 inspiration [ˌɪnspəˈreʃən] (n.) 靈感
7 attend [əˈtɛnd] (v.) 上（學）
8 tuberculosis [tjuˌbɝkjəˈlosɪs] (n.) 結核病

9 windswept [ˈwɪndˌswɛpt] (a.) 迎風的
10 private [ˈpraɪvɪt] (a.) 私人的
11 academy [əˈkædəmɪ] (n.) 學院
12 publish [ˈpʌblɪʃ] (v.) 出版
13 poetry [ˈpoɪtrɪ] (n.)（總稱）詩
14 wuther [ˈwʌðɚ] (v.)〔英〕風呼嘯地吹
15 height [haɪt] (n.) 高處

ABOUT THE BOOK

Wuthering Heights is a story about love and revenge[1]. It follows the life of Heathcliff, a mysterious[2] gypsy[3]-like person, from his childhood to his death at the age of 38. It is set[4] on the moors in West Yorkshire, an area Emily Brontë knew and loved. It is the only novel Brontë ever published.

The title[5] of the book is the name of one of the two houses that feature[6] in the book, and describes[7] the house's position[8] on a windy (wuthering) hill (height). It tells the story of the unresolved[9] love and passion[10] between childhood friends, Catherine Earnshaw and Heathcliff and how it destroys[11] both them and their families.

1 revenge [rɪˋvɛndʒ] (n.) 報仇
2 mysterious [mɪsˋtɪrɪəs] (a.) 神祕的
3 gypsy [ˋdʒɪpsɪ] (n.) 吉普賽人
4 set [sɛt] (v.) 設定 (動詞三態：set; set; set)
5 title [ˋtaɪtl] (n.) 書名
6 feature [ˋfitʃɚ] (v.) 扮演重要角色
7 describe [dɪˋskraɪb] (v.) 描述
8 position [pəˋzɪʃən] (n.) 位置
9 unresolved [͵ʌnrɪˋzɑlvd] (a.) 未解決的
10 passion [ˋpæʃən] (n.) 激情
11 destroy [dɪˋstrɔɪ] (v.) 毀滅
12 flashback [ˋflæʃ͵bæk] (n.) 倒敘
13 narrator [næˋretɚ] (n.) 敘述者
14 grange [grendʒ] (n.) 農莊
15 servant [ˋsɝvənt] (n.) 僕人
16 take part in 參加……
17 account [əˋkaunt] (n.) 描述
18 theme [θim] (n.) 主題

The book is told in a series of flashbacks[12] by two narrators[13]. The first, Mr Lockwood, rents Thrushcross Grange[14] from Heathcliff and the second, Nelly Dean, is a servant[15] who tells Lockwood about the events of the past. Both of the narrators take part in[16] the action of the story and allow us to have a first-hand account[17] of both the present and past.

The main theme[18] in the story is love, and how love can damage people if it is not expressed[19] well. Unresolved love can turn to hate and hate becomes revenge. Nature is another important part of the story and the conflict[20] between nature and civilization[21] is embodied[22] in the relationship between Heathcliff and his rival[23], Edgar Linton.

Although *Wuthering Heights* is now considered to be a classic of English literature[24] when it was first published critics[25] found the book to be strange and shocking yet they all agreed that it was compulsive[26] reading.

---

19 express [ɪkˋsprɛs] (v.) 表達
20 conflict [ˋkɑnflɪkt] (n.) 衝突
21 civilization [ˌsɪvḷəˋzeʃən] (n.) 文明
22 embody [ɪmˋbɑdɪ] (v.) 具體地表現
23 rival [ˋraɪvḷ] (n.) 情敵

24 literature [ˋlɪtərətʃɚ] (n.) 文學
25 critic [ˋkrɪtɪk] (n.) 批評家
26 compulsive [kəmˋpʌlsɪv] (a.)
　　禁不住的

BEFORE READING

1 Look at the family tree of the main characters in the story. Read the sentences and fill in the missing names **1**–**4**.

- ⓐ Catherine and Edgar's daughter is called Cathy Linton.
- ⓑ Hindley married a woman called Frances.
- ⓒ Linton is Heathcliff's son's first name.
- ⓓ Edgar's sister's name is Isabella.

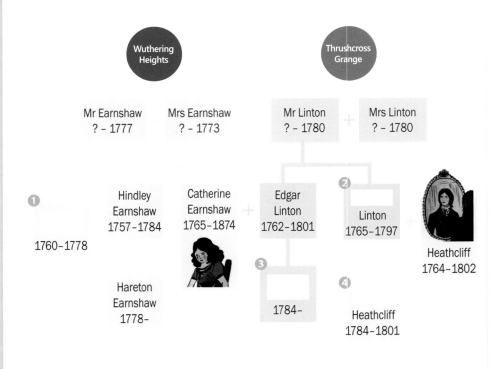

Wuthering Heights

Thrushcross Grange

Mr Earnshaw
? – 1777

Mrs Earnshaw
? – 1773

Mr Linton
? – 1780

Mrs Linton
? – 1780

1
1760–1778

Hindley Earnshaw
1757–1784

Catherine Earnshaw
1765–1874

Edgar Linton
1762–1801

2
Linton
1765–1797

Heathcliff
1764–1802

Hareton Earnshaw
1778–

3
1784–

4
Heathcliff
1784–1801

2 Create your own family tree. Ask your family for the information. Compare family trees with a partner.

3 Look again at the information in the family tree in Exercise **1**.
Answer the questions.

- a How many cousins did Cathy Linton have?
- b How old was Hindley Earnshaw when he died?
- c Which two characters died in 1780? And which two in 1801?
- d Who was younger – Heathcliff or Edgar Linton?
- e What was the relationship between Hareton Earnshaw and Edgar Linton?

4 The following sentences describe 5 of the characters.
Match a beginning (a-e) with a suitable ending (1-5).

_____ a Heathcliff had dark hair and eyes and dressed
_____ b Cathy Linton had golden curls that fell
_____ c Hareton's hair was uncombed and his hands were brown
_____ d Catherine Earnshaw had thick dark curls, dark eyes
_____ e Linton Heathcliff was a delicate boy

- 1 over her shoulders.
- 2 with a pale, sad face.
- 3 and a passionate nature.
- 4 like a gentleman.
- 5 from working outside.

5 Look at the pictures in the book. Which of the characters in Exercise **3** can you see on these pages?

A

B

6 Read about the two houses where most of the events in the story take place. Look at the pictures below. Which of the photos are most like the description?

_____ ⓐ **Wuthering Heights:** a sixteenth century farmhouse situated on the top of a hill. "Wuthering" means "stormy" or "windy" in the local language. After Thrushcross Grange it is the best building in the neighborhood.

_____ ⓑ **Thrushcross Grange:** the most important building in the neighborhood. It is an elegant house situated in a large park and is about six and a half kilometers from Wuthering Heights.

7 Write descriptions of the other two houses.

8 Number the events in the story in the order you think they happen.

_____ a Heathcliff runs away from Wuthering Heights and makes a lot of money.

_____ b Heathcliff and Catherine become close friends.

_____ c Heathcliff becomes the owner of Thrushcross Grange.

_____ d Heathcliff goes to visit Catherine for the last time before she dies.

_____ e Heathcliff arranges the marriage of his son to Catherine's daughter.

9 Choose suitable words from the box that describe the feelings shown in the events below.

| 1. hate | 2. love | 3. sadness | 4. sympathy | 5. violence |

_____ a Nelly felt sorry for Heathcliff because Hindley was cruel to him.

_____ b Heathcliff was determined to take his revenge on Hindley.

_____ c Heathcliff and Catherine cried when old Mr Earnshaw died.

_____ d Hindley and Heathcliff had a fight when Hindley tried to stab Heathcliff with a knife.

_____ e Cathy went back to Wuthering Heights because of her feelings for Linton.

10 Discuss the following questions about friendship and love with a partner.

a How does friendship between people grow and become stronger?

b What are the similarities and differences between friendship and love?

1. A Visitor at Wuthering Heights

I have been to see my landlord[1] Mr Heathcliff today. He's my only neighbor here in this beautiful but wild part of England.

He was standing at the gate to his farm when I arrived. His black eyes looked at me suspiciously[2].

"Mr Heathcliff?" I said.

He nodded[3].

"I am Mr Lockwood, your new tenant[4] at Thrushcross Grange, sir."

"Come in!" he said coldly, opening the gate.

I'm not a sociable man but I had the impression[5] that Mr Heathcliff was even less sociable[6] than me.

I rode through the gate and he followed me up the small road to the house. As we entered[7] the courtyard[8] he shouted to an old man, "Joseph! Take Mr Lockwood's horse and bring us some wine."

The name of Mr Heathcliff's house is Wuthering Heights. "Wuthering" means "stormy" or "windy" in the local language and it describes the place well. The house stands on the top of a hill. On one side of it there are a few trees. They all lean[9] in the same direction, blown[10] by the strong north winds.

---

1 landlord ['lænd,lɔrd] (n.) 房東
2 suspiciously [sə'spɪʃəslɪ] (adv.) 狐疑地
3 nod [nɑd] (v.) 點頭
4 tenant ['tɛnənt] (n.) 承租人
5 impression [ɪm'prɛʃən] (n.) 印象
6 sociable ['soʃəbl̩] (a.) 善交際的

7 enter ['ɛntə] (v.) 進入
8 courtyard ['kort'jɑrd] (n.) 庭院
9 lean [lin] (v.) 傾斜（動詞三態：
  lean; leaned, leant; leaned, leant）
10 blow [blo] (v.) 吹（動詞三態：
  blow; blew; blown）

We went into the sitting room[1]. The floor was made of smooth[2], white stone. There was a big fireplace[3] at one end of it and a large dresser[4] at the other end. Several large hunting dogs were lying in the dark corners of the room.

It was a simple, pleasant room, a farmer's room. Mr Heathcliff seemed out of place[5] there. He doesn't look like a farmer. He's a tall, handsome man, very dark like a gypsy, but he dresses like a gentleman. The expression[6] on his face is cold and hard, perhaps cruel. I might be wrong of course.

I sat down in one of the chairs near the fire and he stood opposite[7] me. One of the dogs, a female, came up to me and I put out my hand to touch her. She snarled[8], showing her teeth.

"Best not to touch her," growled[9] Mr Heathcliff. "She isn't a pet."

Then he walked over to the door and shouted to the old man again, "Joseph!"

There was no sign[10] of the servant so Heathcliff went to look for[11] him. He left me alone with the dogs. I sat quietly and looked at them for a while[12]. Then suddenly[13] the female[14] dog jumped on me. I tried to push her away but the other dogs ran over and joined her.

I shouted for help and a large woman with a frying pan[15] ran in. She hit[16] the dogs with the frying pan and shouted at them. They were afraid of her and went silently[17] back to their dark corners.

---

1 sitting room 起居室
2 smooth [smuð] (a.) 平滑的
3 fireplace [ˈfaɪrˌples] (n.) 壁爐
4 dresser [ˈdrɛsɚ] (n.) 餐具櫥
5 out of place 不合適
6 expression [ɪkˈsprɛʃən] (n.) 表情
7 opposite [ˈɑpəzɪt] (prep.) 在對面

8 snarl [ˈsnɑrl] (v.) 吠
9 growl [graʊl] (v.) 咆哮
10 sign [saɪn] (n.) 跡象
11 look for 尋找
12 for a while 一會兒
13 suddenly [ˈsʌdṇlɪ] (adv.) 突然地
14 female [ˈfimel] (a.) 母的

At that moment Heathcliff came back.

"What's going on?" he asked angrily.

"Your dogs are as wild as tigers!" I said. "They aren't safe to leave with strangers."

"They're hunting dogs," he replied[18]. "Here! Have a glass of wine!"

"No, thank you," I replied coldly.

"Come on, Mr Lockwood! Don't be angry," Heathcliff said. "Drink some wine. We don't have guests very often here. My dogs and I have forgotten how to receive[19] them."

I tried to forget my anger and we started talking. To my surprise, I enjoyed our conversation very much.

When it was time for me to leave I said, "I'll come and see you again tomorrow".

He didn't seem to like the idea but that wasn't going to stop me.

HEATHCLIFF

- Why did Mr Heathcliff's appearance[20] surprise Mr Lockwood?
- What kind of life do you think Mr Heathcliff leads[21] ?
- What do you think will happen the next time Mr Lockwood visits Wuthering Heights?

15 frying pan

16 hit [hɪt] (v.) 打（動詞三態：hit; hit; hit）

17 silently [ˈsaɪləntlɪ] (adv.) 安靜地

18 reply [rɪˈplaɪ] (v.) 回答

19 receive [rɪˈsiv] (v.) 款待

20 appearance [əˈpɪrəns] (n.) 外貌

21 lead a...life 過著……的生活

I set out[1] after lunch the following day. It was cold and the sky was gray. A few snowflakes[2] were falling as I knocked at the door of Wuthering Heights.

There was no reply. I knocked again and shook[3] the latch[4].

Hearing the noise, Joseph came to the barn[5] door.

"The master[6] is in the fields," he shouted.

"Is there nobody at home?" I replied.

"Only the mistress[7] and she never opens the door," he said and went back inside the barn.

It was snowing heavily now and I was very cold. I tried to open the door but it was locked.

Suddenly a young man appeared in the courtyard. He made a sign with his hand telling me to follow him.

We went to the back of the house and through the kitchen to the sitting room. A big fire was burning in the fireplace and there were cups and plates[8] on the table. A girl was sitting near it.

"She must be the mistress of the house," I thought.

She looked at me in a cool, disinterested[9] way but didn't say anything. I felt very uncomfortable[10].

"Sit down! He'll be back soon," said the young man. His manner[11] wasn't very welcoming.

---

1 set out 動身
2 snowflake [ˋsno͵flek] (n.) 雪花
3 shake [ʃek] (v.) 搖（動詞三態：shake; shook; shaken）
4 latch [lætʃ] (n.) 門閂
5 barn [bɑrn] (n.) 馬房

6 master [ˋmæstɚ] (n.) 主人
7 mistress [ˋmɪstrɪs] (n.) 女主人
8 plate [plet] (n.) 盤子
9 disinterested [dɪsˋɪntərɪstɪd] (a.) 冷漠的
10 uncomfortable [ʌnˋkʌmfɚtəbl̩] (a.) 不舒服的
11 manner [ˋmænɚ] (n.) 態度

I could see the girl well now. She was about seventeen, slim[1] and very pretty. Her hair was the color of gold and fell over her shoulders. Her eyes were beautiful but there was a disagreeable[2] expression in them.

The young man was looking at me angrily. I couldn't decide if he was a servant or not. He was dressed like one and he spoke like one. His thick brown curls[3] were uncombed[4] and his hands and face were brown from working outside. But his manner was proud and free, not like a servant's.

Neither of them spoke to me and I was glad when, a few minutes later, Heathcliff walked in.

"I have come, sir, as I promised[5]!" I said. "And I'm afraid I'll have to stay here until the snow stops. Perhaps one of your servants will take me home later."

"They are all too busy," he replied. Then he turned to the young girl and said, "Get the tea ready!"

We pulled our chairs to the table while the girl poured[6] the tea.

We drank our tea in silence and there was a very tense[7] atmosphere[8] in the room. I thought it was my fault[9] so I tried to be sociable.

"This is a beautiful part of the country," I said, "but very isolated[10]. However, you seem very happy here, with your wife and family..."

"My wife!" Heathcliff exclaimed[11] looking around him. "Where? Are you talking about her spirit[12]?"

---

1 slim [slɪm] (n.) 纖瘦的
2 disagreeable [ˌdɪsəˈɡriəbl̩] (a.) 不愉快的
3 curl [kɝl] (n.) 捲髮
4 uncombed [ʌmˈkomd] (a.) 蓬亂的

5 promise [ˈprɑmɪs] (v.) 承諾
6 pour [por] (v.) 倒
7 tense [tɛns] (a.) 緊張的
8 atmosphere [ˈætməsˌfɪr] (n.) 氣氛

How stupid of me! Of course the girl wasn't his wife! She was much too young for him. She must be married[13] to the young man.

"Mrs Heathcliff is my daughter-in-law,[14]" said Heathcliff, reading my thoughts. There was hatred[15] on his face as he spoke.

"Ah, yes," I said. "You are very lucky to have such a lovely wife, young man."

The youth[16] went red and looked down at his plate.

"I said she was my daughter-in-law, sir. She was married to my son," said Heathcliff.

"And this young man is…"

"Not my son."

"My name is Hareton Earnshaw," growled the youth angrily.

The atmosphere began to depress[17] me and I promised myself not to make a third visit to Wuthering Heights.

After a long silence I asked, "Perhaps one of your servants is free now to take me home?"

"There's only Heathcliff, Hareton, Zillah the housekeeper[18], Joseph and me here," said the girl.

"Then I suppose I'll have to stay until the morning," I replied.

"You'll have to share a bed with Hareton or Joseph, if you do," Heathcliff said rudely[19]. Although he dressed like a gentleman, he certainly didn't behave[20] like one.

---

9 fault [fɔlt] (n.) 過失
10 isolated [ˋaɪslˌetɪd] (a.) 孤立的
11 exclaim [ɪksˋklem] (v.) 大聲叫嚷
12 spirit [ˋspɪrɪt] (n.) 鬼魂
13 marry [ˋmærɪ] (v.) 結婚
14 daughter-in-law [ˋdɔtərɪnˌlɔ] (n.) 媳婦

15 hatred [ˋhetrɪd] (n.) 憎恨；敵意
16 youth [juθ] (n.) 年輕人
17 depress [dɪˋprɛs] (v.) 使沮喪
18 housekeeper [ˋhausˌkipə] (n.) 管家
19 rudely [ˋrudlɪ] (adv.) 無禮地
20 behave [bɪˋhev] (v.) 行為舉止

I felt very angry with all of them. I stood up, pushed past[1] Heathcliff and ran out into the dark courtyard. There was a lantern[2] near the door. I picked it up and rushed[3] towards the gate.

Suddenly two hairy monsters[4] flew[5] at my throat, knocking me down. They sat on me until Heathcliff and Hareton arrived and pulled them off.

I was so frightened that my nose started to bleed[6]. Hearing the noise, Zillah came out. She quickly poured some icy water down my neck and pulled me into the kitchen.

I felt weak[7] and couldn't stand up. Heathcliff told Zillah to find me a bed for the night.

LOCKWOOD

- Imagine you are Lockwood. How do you feel? Tell a partner.

1 push past 從（某人）身邊擠過去
2 lantern [ˈlæntɚn] (n.) 提燈
3 rush [rʌʃ] (v.) 衝
4 monster [ˈmɑnstɚ] (n.) 怪物
5 fly [flaɪ] (v.) 飛（動詞三態：fly; flew; flown）
6 bleed [blid] (v.) 流血（動詞三態：bleed; bled; bled）
7 weak [wik] (a.) 虛弱的

2. A Ghost at the Window

Zillah took me upstairs to a bedroom.

"Don't make a noise!" she said. "The master doesn't usually allow people to stay in this room."

"Why not?" I asked.

"I don't know," she replied. "I've only been here a couple of[1] years. A lot of strange things happen in this house," she added. "I don't ask questions anymore."

I closed the door and got into bed. I put my candle on a small shelf[2] next to a pile[3] of old books. To my surprise I saw that the shelf was covered in writing. Three names were scratched[4] in the paint[5]: Catherine Earnshaw, Catherine Heathcliff and Catherine Linton.

I looked at them until my eyes began to close and I fell asleep[6]. A few minutes later the white letters of the names started jumping out of the darkness and I woke up suddenly.

"I'll read for a while," I thought and I picked up one of the books on the shelf.

It was a diary. On the first page I read, "Catherine Earnshaw, her book", and a date of twenty-five years ago. Curious[7] to know more about this Catherine, I started to read.

CATHERINE

- Who do you think the three Catherines are?
- How might Catherine Earnshaw be related to[8] Hareton Earnshaw?

On one of the pages there was a description[9] of a Sunday at Wuthering Heights. I understood the following: Catherine Earnshaw's father was dead and she lived with her cruel older brother Hindley.

Although I was very sleepy, I read a few more pages. It gradually[10] became clear that Catherine and Heathcliff were close friends, and that Hindley and his young wife Frances hated Heathcliff.

---

1 a couple of 兩個
2 shelf [ʃɛlf] (n.) 架子
3 pile [paɪl] (n.) 堆
4 scratch [skrætʃ] (v.) 亂劃
5 paint [pent] (n.) 漆

6 fall asleep 睡著
7 curious [ˋkjʊrɪəs] (a.) 好奇的
8 be related to 有關
9 description [dɪˋskrɪpʃən] (n.) 描繪
10 gradually [ˋgrædʒʊəlɪ] (adv.) 漸漸地

(11)   Then I lay[1] my head on the pillow and fell asleep again. I had terrible dreams that night. There was a lot of noise – rapping[2] and tapping[3] sounds. I woke up.

The branch[4] of a tree outside was hitting the glass in the window. I turned over and went back to sleep. But the rapping sound continued in my dream. I decided to stop it.

I got up, pushed my hand through the glass and put out my arm. But, instead of the branch, my fingers closed on a little ice-cold hand. The hand held mine tightly and a sad voice sobbed[5], "Let me in!"

"Who are you?" I said.

"Catherine Linton," it replied. "I've come home. I lost my way on the moor! Let me in!"

"How can I?" I said. "You must let me go if you want me to let you in!"

The fingers relaxed and I pulled my hand back through the window and put some books in front of the broken glass.

I listened and the voice cried again, "Let me in!"

"Go away!" I shouted.

The hand outside scratched on the window. I tried to get up but I couldn't move. I shouted again in fright[6]. Then I heard footsteps outside the door and somebody pushed it open.

"Is there anyone inside?" a voice said.

---

1 lie [laɪ] (v.) 躺（動詞三態：lie; lay; lain）
2 rapping [ˋræpɪŋ] (a.) 猛擊的
3 tapping [ˋtæpɪŋ] (a.) 輕擊的
4 branch [bræntʃ] (n.) 樹枝
5 sob [sɑb] (v.) 嗚咽；啜泣
6 fright [fraɪt] (n.) 驚嚇

I sat up. I was shaking and sweating[1]. It was Heathcliff. He was standing at the door in his shirt and trousers holding a candle. His face was as white as the wall behind him.

"It's only me, sir," I called out. "Lockwood. I was having a very bad dream and I screamed[2] in my sleep. I'm sorry I disturbed[3] you."

"Why are you sleeping in this room?" he said angrily. "Who brought you here? Tell me!"

"It was your servant Zillah," I replied. I got out of bed and started to dress. "Perhaps she wants to prove that the house is haunted[4]. Well, it is! It's full of ghosts[5]!"

"What do you mean?" asked Heathcliff. "And what are you doing? Go back to bed and don't repeat that horrible noise."

"I'm going to walk in the courtyard until morning, and then I'll go home," I said. "And don't worry! I'm not going to come back!"

"Take the candle, and go where you like," he muttered[6]. "I'll join you in two minutes!"

I left the room but stopped outside the door because I didn't know which way to go.

Not realizing[7] that I was still there, Heathcliff got on the bed and pulled the window open. Then he burst into tears[8].

"Come in, come in!" he sobbed. "Catherine, come in! Oh, my darling!"

---

1 sweat [swɛt] (v.) 流汗（動詞三態：sweat; sweat, sweated; sweat, sweated）
2 scream [skrim] (v.) 尖叫
3 disturb [dɪsˋtɝb] (v.) 打擾
4 haunted [ˋhɔntɪd] (a.) 鬧鬼的
5 ghost [gost] (n.) 鬼
6 mutter [ˋmʌtɚ] (v.) 低聲嘀咕
7 realize [ˋrɪəˏlaɪz] (v.) 認識到
8 burst into tears 突然哭出來
9 park [pɑrk] (n.) 鄉村宅第四周的林園

CATHERINE

- How do you think Heathcliff feels about Catherine?

I didn't want to embarrass him so I went downstairs.

I waited in the kitchen until it began to get light and then escaped into the cold air of the morning.

As I was crossing the garden, my landlord called to me and offered to take me across the moor. I'm glad he did because the snow was like a white ocean and it was impossible to see the road.

We didn't speak much on the way to Thrushcross Grange and he left me at the gates to the park[9]. The distance from the gates to the house is only two miles but I got lost several times. The clock was chiming[10] twelve as I entered the house.

My housekeeper Mrs Dean was happy to see me.

"We were worried," she said. "It's easy to get lost on the moor in the snow."

I changed my clothes and I went down to my study. There was a cheerful[11] fire in the fireplace and some hot coffee on the table. I sat down in my armchair[12] feeling very weak and tired after my bad night and long walk across the moor.

10 chime [tʃaɪm] (v.) 鳴鐘報時
11 cheerful [ˋtʃɪrfəl] (a.) 熊熊的（火）
12 armchair [ˋɑrmˏtʃɛr] (n.) 扶手椅

3. The Earnshaws

I came to live at Thrushcross Grange because I wanted to be alone. I didn't want to have to talk to anyone. But after a few hours in my study I began to feel very sad and lonely. So, when Mrs Dean brought in my supper, I asked her to stay and talk to me. She agreed and went to get her sewing[1].

When she was sitting comfortably, I said, "You've lived here a long time, haven't you, Mrs Dean? Sixteen years I think."

"Eighteen, sir. I came when the mistress married. After she died, the master asked me to be his housekeeper."

She paused[2].

"Ah! Times have changed since then!"

"Yes," I said. "I suppose[3] they have."

I was curious to know the history of the people at Wuthering Heights. "Mrs Dean must know it," I thought. I decided to introduce[4] the subject[5].

"Why does Heathcliff live at Wuthering Heights and not at Thrushcross Grange?" I asked. "Thrushcross Grange is much more comfortable. Isn't he rich enough?"

"Rich, sir!" she said. "He has enough money to live in a much better house than this one. But he doesn't like spending his money. It's strange because he's alone in the world."

"He had a son, didn't he?"

1 sewing [ˈsoɪŋ] (n.) 針線活
2 pause [pɔz] (v.) 暫停
3 suppose [səˈpoz] (v.) 猜想
4 introduce [ˌɪntrəˈdjus] (v.) 引出
5 subject [ˈsʌbdʒɪkt] (n.) 話題
6 widow [ˈwɪdo] (n.) 寡婦
7 late [let] (a.) 已故的

"Yes, he did, but his son died."

"And that young lady, Mrs Heathcliff, is the son's widow[6]?"

"Yes."

"Where's she from?"

"From Thrushcross Grange, sir! She's the daughter of Mr Linton, my late[7] master. Catherine Linton was her name before she married."

"What! Catherine Linton?" I exclaimed. (But no! It was impossible that she was the same girl as my ghost of the previous night.)

"So," I continued, "your master was called Linton?"

"Yes, sir," she replied. Then she put her sewing down and asked, "How is Cathy?"

"Mrs Heathcliff? She looked very well. But I don't think she's very happy."

"Oh dear! I'm not surprised to hear that. And what did you think of the master?"

"He's a hard man, Mrs Dean. And a rude one, too."

"Yes, he is."

"Do you know anything about his past?"

"I know a lot about it although I don't know anything about his parents or where his fortune[1] came from."

"And who is that boy, Earnshaw?"

"Hareton Earnshaw is the young lady's cousin. Her husband was her cousin, too. One on the mother's side, the other on the father's side. Heathcliff married Mr Linton's sister, you see. Poor Hareton! He doesn't know that Heathcliff cheated[2] him. Heathcliff took all of his property[3]."

"Well, Mrs Dean, I won't be able to rest if you don't tell me more about my neighbors. Please tell me more."

She seemed very happy to do this and began her story.

Nelly Dean's story:

Before I came to live here, I spent a lot of time at Wuthering Heights. My mother looked after[4] Hindley Earnshaw, Hareton's father. Hindley and I were the same age. His sister Catherine was eight years younger than us.

One day old Mr Earnshaw went to Liverpool on business[5]. He was away for three days and when he came back he brought a child with him. The child wasn't very old, about Catherine's age, but he was dirty and dressed in rags[6]. He looked like a gypsy. They called him "Heathcliff".

Not long after that, Mrs Earnshaw died and the three children were left without a mother.

---

1 fortune ['fɔrtʃən] (n.) 財富
2 cheat [tʃit] (v.) 詐騙
3 property ['prɑpətɪ] (n.) 財產
4 look after 照顧

BROTHERS AND SISTERS

- Work with a partner. Discuss the advantages[7] and disadvantages[8] of having brothers and sisters. Make notes. Compare your ideas with the rest of the class.
- Take a vote[9] on whether you think it's better to have brothers and sisters or to be an only child.

Catherine and Heathcliff became close friends but Hindley always hated him. I must say, I didn't like him much either. He was a strange child. He never complained or cried when Hindley hit him. Old Mr Earnshaw was furious[10] when he discovered that his son was persecuting[11] the boy. Heathcliff was definitely[12] his favorite.

I often wondered why Mr Earnshaw admired[13] him. Heathcliff never showed any signs of affection[14] for the old man or any signs of gratitude[15] either. But the old man's love gave him power over Hindley.

I remember Mr Earnshaw once bought a couple of young horses and gave one to each of the boys. Heathcliff took the best one but it hurt its leg. He wanted to exchange[16] it for Hindley's.

---

5 on business 出差
6 in rags 衣衫襤褸
7 advantage [əd`væntɪdʒ] (n.) 優點
8 disadvantage [ˌdɪsəd`væntɪdʒ] (n.) 缺點
9 vote [vot] (n.) 投票
10 furious [`fjʊərɪəs] (a.) 狂怒的

11 persecute [`pɝsɪˌkjut] (v.) 迫害
12 definitely [`dɛfənɪtlɪ] (adv.) 明確地
13 admire [əd`maɪr] (v.) 欣賞
14 affection [ə`fɛkʃən] (n.) 情感
15 gratitude [`ɡrætəˌtjud] (n.) 感激之情
16 exchange [ɪks`tʃendʒ] (v.) 交換

18 "You must give me your horse," he said. "I don't like mine. If you don't, I'll tell your father about how you hit and beat me."

Hindley picked up an iron[1] bar[2] saying, "Get away from me!"

"Throw[3] it!" replied Heathcliff not moving. "I'll also tell him that you're going to send me away as soon as he dies."

Hindley threw the bar and it hit Heathcliff on the chest. He fell down, but got up again immediately. His face was white but he looked calmly at Hindley.

"Take my horse then, gypsy!" shouted Hindley. "And I hope he kicks you!"

Heathcliff was passing behind the animal to change saddles[4] when suddenly Hindley pushed him. Heathcliff fell under the horse's feet. Hindley ran away as fast as he could.

Heathcliff didn't say anything. He got up and rested for a while to recover[5] from the blow[6].

Then he went into the house. He didn't show the mark[7] on his chest to Mr Earnshaw and I thought it was because he wasn't a vindictive[8] boy. But I was wrong, as you will hear.

---

1 iron [ˋaɪən] (adj.) 鐵的
2 bar [bɑr] (n.) 棒
3 throw [θro] (v.) 擲（動詞三態：throw; threw; thrown）
4 saddle [ˋsædl̩] (n.) 馬鞍
5 recover [rɪˋkʌvə] (v.) 恢復
6 blow [blo] (n.) 重擊
7 mark [mɑrk] (n.) 痕跡
8 vindictive [vɪnˋdɪktɪv] (a.) 懷恨的

4. The Lintons

Nelly Dean continued her story:

As Mr Earnshaw got older and weaker, he became bad-tempered[1]. Hindley often made him angry by saying nasty[2] things about Heathcliff. Once or twice the old man lifted[3] his stick[4] to hit his son but he was too weak to do it. Then he shook with rage[5].

In the end the local curate[6] advised him to send Hindley away to school. Mr Earnshaw agreed but he was sad to see his son leave. I wasn't.

"Maybe we'll have some peace now," I thought.

Catherine was still at home. She was a very pretty girl with thick dark curls and dark eyes and a passionate[7] nature. She talked, sang and laughed from the moment she got up to the moment she went to bed. She liked to play the mistress of the house, giving Hindley, Heathcliff and me orders. When the boys didn't obey[8] her, she hit them. But I never let her hit me.

She was very fond of[9] Heathcliff – too fond. The worst punishment[10] we could invent[11] for her was to keep them separate[12].

---

1 bad-tempered [ˈbædˈtɛmpəd] (a.) 脾氣不好的
2 nasty [ˈnæstɪ] (a.) 卑鄙的
3 lift [lɪft] (v.) 舉起
4 stick [stɪk] (n.) 拐杖
5 rage [redʒ] (n.) 狂怒
6 curate [ˈkjʊrɪt] (n.) 副牧師
7 passionate [ˈpæʃənɪt] (a.) 熱烈的
8 obey [əˈbe] (v.) 聽從
9 be fond of 喜歡
10 punishment [ˈpʌnɪʃmənt] (n.) 懲罰
11 invent [ɪnˈvɛnt] (v.) 發明；創造
12 separate [ˈsɛpəˌret] (a.) 分開的

Then one October evening Mr Earnshaw died quietly in his chair. Both Catherine and Heathcliff were very upset[1]. They cried and cried. I didn't have time to comfort them because I had to go to the village to get the doctor.

When I came back I went straight to their room. It was after midnight but they weren't asleep. They were comforting each other by describing all the beautiful things in heaven[2]. Tears ran down my face as I listened to them.

Hindley came home for his father's funeral[3] and brought a wife with him! We were all amazed[4]. She was young and pretty but very thin. Her eyes sparkled[5] like diamonds[6]. Her name was Frances. She trembled[7] a lot and cried at the funeral. She said she was afraid of dying. Later I noticed she breathed[8] with difficulty when she climbed the stairs.

At first Frances was very happy to have a new sister but her enthusiasm[9] for Catherine didn't last long. She didn't like Heathcliff at all. She didn't want him in the sitting room so Hindley sent him to sit in the kitchen with the servants. He also stopped Heathcliff's lessons with the curate and made him work outside in the fields with the farm boys.

Heathcliff didn't mind at first, because Catherine taught him what she learnt. She also worked or played with him in the fields. They were growing up like wild savages[10] because nobody looked after them.

---

1 upset [ʌpˋsɛt] (a.) 難過的
2 heaven [ˋhɛvən] (n.) 天堂
3 funeral [ˋfjunərəl] (n.) 葬禮
4 amazed [əˋmezd] (a.) 吃驚的
5 sparkle [ˋspɑrk!] (v.) 閃耀
6 diamond [ˋdaɪəmənd] (n.) 鑽石
7 tremble [ˋtrɛmb!] (v.) 顫抖
8 breathe [brið] (v.) 呼吸
9 enthusiasm [ɪnˋθjuzɪ,æzəm] (n.) 熱情
10 savage [ˋsævɪdʒ] (n.) 野蠻人

They loved running around the moor. Sometimes they went there in the morning and stayed away all day. They were punished for it but it didn't matter. They forgot everything as soon as they were together again.

PUNISHMENT

- Catherine and Heathcliff were punished for going onto the moor. What forms of discipline[1] are used in your school?
- Do you think they work? Have you ever been disciplined? Why? Share your ideas in groups of four.

One Sunday evening they were sent out of the sitting room for making a noise. When I went to call them to supper, I couldn't find them anywhere. We searched[2] the house, upstairs and downstairs, and the courtyard too, but they weren't there. Hindley was furious.

"Lock the doors!" he said. "Don't let them in when they come back!"

We went to bed but I couldn't sleep because I was too worried. I opened my window and listened for them. After a while I heard footsteps[3] and saw the light of a lantern in the road. It was Heathcliff. He was alone. I ran down to open the door.

"Where's Miss Catherine?" I cried. "Has she had an accident[4]?"

"She's at Thrushcross Grange," he answered. "They didn't want me to stay so I had to come back."

"Well, you're in trouble[5] now!" I said. "But what were you doing at Thrushcross Grange?"

"Let me take off my wet clothes and I'll tell you all about it, Nelly," he replied.

While he was changing, he told me what happened.

"Catherine and I went for a walk on the moor. We saw the lights at the Grange and we decided to go and look through the windows.

We ran down the hill and hid under the sitting room window. The light was on. Inside we saw – ah! it was beautiful, Nelly! – a wonderful place.

The carpet was red, the chairs and tables were covered with red cloth[6] and the ceiling was pure white with a gold border[7]. A beautiful light with glass drops[8] and silver chains hung from the center.

Edgar and his sister were alone. What do you think they were doing? Isabella – I think she's eleven, a year younger than Catherine – was lying on the floor screaming[9] at one end of the room. Edgar was standing near the fireplace crying quietly at the other. They were quarreling[10] over a little dog that was sitting in the middle of the table.

---

1 discipline [ˈdɪsəplɪn] (n.) 懲戒
2 search [sɜtʃ] (v.) 尋找
3 footstep [ˈfʊtˌstɛp] (n.) 腳步聲
4 accident [ˈæksədənt] (n.) 意外
5 in trouble 惹上麻煩

6 cloth [klɔθ] (n.) 布
7 border [ˈbɔrdə] (n.) 邊緣
8 drop [drɑp] (n.) 滴狀物
9 scream [skrim] (v.) 尖叫
10 quarrel [ˈkwɔrəl] (v.) 爭吵

The idiots! We laughed loudly at them but then they heard us. They were scared[1] and started shouting, 'Mama! Papa!'

Someone opened the front door so we started to run. I was holding Catherine's hand when she suddenly fell down.

'Run, Heathcliff, run!' she whispered[2]. 'They've let the dog out, and he's holding me!'

The dog had her ankle in its mouth, Nelly, but she didn't cry. Then a servant arrived with a lantern. He pulled the dog away from Catherine and picked her up[3]. She was in great pain. He carried[4] her into the house and I followed.

'What's going on?' asked Mr Linton.

'We have caught a little girl, sir,' said the servant. 'And there's a boy here, too.'

Mr Linton pulled me under the beautiful light and the two children came closer.

'Horrible[5] thing!' said Isabella. 'Put him in the cellar[6], Papa.'

Edgar was looking at Catherine.

'That's Miss Earnshaw,' he whispered to his mother. 'I've seen her at church. Look at her foot! It's bleeding!'

'Miss Earnshaw? Nonsense[7]!' cried Mrs Linton. She looked at Catherine more closely. 'But you're right, Edgar. It is Miss Earnshaw!' she exclaimed. 'Why is she running around the moor with a gypsy?'

---

1 scared [skɛrd] (a.) 嚇壞的
2 whisper [ˋhwɪspɚ] (v.) 低聲説
3 pick up 救起某人
4 carry [ˋkærɪ] (v.) 抱起
5 horrible [ˋhɔrəbl̩] (a.) 可怕的
6 cellar [ˋsɛlɚ] (n.) 地下室
7 nonsense [ˋnɑnsɛns] (int.) 胡説

'He isn't a gypsy,' said her husband. 'Mr Earnshaw found him in Liverpool and brought him here.'

'A wicked[1] boy, probably,' said his wife. 'I don't want him in my house. Take him away, Robert!'

I didn't want to leave without Catherine but the servant pushed me into the garden and told me to go home. I had to leave her there, Nelly."

1 wicked ['wɪkɪd] (a.) 壞的

5. A Rival for Heathcliff

Nelly Dean continued her story:

Catherine stayed at Thrushcross Grange for five weeks, until Christmas. She was no longer a wild girl when she came back – she was a lady. She had a hat with a feather[1] and her brown hair fell in smooth curls over her shoulders.

When he saw her, Hindley exclaimed: "Catherine! You look lovely! She's more beautiful than Isabella Linton now, isn't she, Frances?"

I helped her take off her cloak[2]. Under it she was wearing a lovely silk dress. She didn't let the dogs come near her because she didn't want them to dirty it.

"Where's Heathcliff?" she demanded[3].

He was hiding in a corner. He was shocked by this beautiful young lady. She didn't look like the Catherine he knew. When she saw him, she ran up to him and kissed him six or seven times. Then she stopped and laughed.

"How very angry you look!" she exclaimed. "And how strange and serious! Well, Heathcliff, have you forgotten me?"

"Go on! Shake hands, Heathcliff," said Hindley, laughing.

"No! I won't," replied the boy. "You're making fun of[4] me!" And he turned to run away but Catherine caught him by the arm.

1 feather [ˈfɛðɚ]   2 cloak [klok]

"I wasn't making fun of you," she said. "But you look strange. You're so dirty!"

"I'll be as dirty as I want. I like being dirty!" Heathcliff said, and he quickly left the room.

Later that evening as I sat in the kitchen, I remembered old Mr Earnshaw's fondness[5] for Heathcliff. I remembered, too, that he was always worried about the boy's future. I thought of Heathcliff's situation[6] now and it made me cry.

"I must help him," I said to myself and so I went out into the courtyard to look for him. He was brushing[7] Catherine's pony[8] in the stable.

"Hurry up, Heathcliff!" I said. "Put on some smart[9] clothes. I'll help you dress. Then when Miss Catherine comes down, you can sit together and chat till bedtime."

He continued brushing the pony and didn't answer me so I went back inside.

He came in later and went straight to his room.

He got up early the next morning and went out on the moor.

The family were still at church. When he came back, he seemed to be happier.

"Nelly," he said. "Make me look nice. I'm going to be good."

"I'm glad to hear it, Heathcliff," I said. "You upset Catherine. She's probably sorry she came home."

"Did she say she was upset?" he asked looking very serious.

---

3 demand [dɪˋmænd] (v.) 質問
4 make fun of 取笑某人
5 fondness [ˋfʌdnɪs] (n.) 喜愛
6 situation [ˏsɪtʃuˋeʃən] (n.) 處境

7 brush [brʌʃ] (v.) 刷
8 pony [ˋponɪ] (n.) 小馬
9 smart [smɑrt] (a.) 華麗的；時髦的

"She cried when I told her you weren't here this morning."

"Well, I cried last night," he replied. "And I had a good reason to cry."

"Yes," I said. "You went to bed without any dinner! But go and wash now. When you're clean and wearing your best clothes, you'll look more handsome than Edgar Linton."

As he was putting on his clean clothes he said to me: "Edgar Linton has light hair and fair[1] skin, Nelly. I'm dark. And he dresses and behaves better than me. He'll be rich one day. I won't!"

"But you are taller, stronger and braver than him, Heathcliff," I replied. "He's weak and afraid of everything. Look at yourself in the mirror! Don't you think you are handsome? Maybe your father was an emperor[2] of China and your mother an Indian queen! Perhaps they had enough money to buy both Wuthering Heights and Thrushcross Grange! Maybe you were kidnapped[3] by sailors and brought to England. If you believe something like that, you'll feel better about yourself and Hindley's insults will be easier to bear[4]."

YOU AND OTHERS

- Write some sentences. Compare yourself with other people you know. e.g.
  - I'm taller than my brother.
  - I'm better at math than my friend Tom.
  - My eyes are more beautiful than my cousin Maria's.

1 fair [fɛr] (a.) 白皙的
2 emperor [ˋɛmpərə] (n.) 皇帝
3 kidnap [ˋkɪdnæp] (v.) 綁架
4 bear [bɛr] (v.) 忍受（動詞三態：
  bear; bore; borne）

Suddenly we heard the sound of a carriage in the courtyard. He went to the window and I hurried to the door to open it.

It was the two Lintons, Hindley, Frances and Catherine. They all ran into the house and stood in front of the large fire in the sitting room to get warm.

I told Heathcliff to go and join them.

He opened the kitchen door as Hindley was coming out of the sitting room. When Hindley saw him, he pushed him back into the kitchen saying, "Joseph! Keep him away from the sitting room!"

Then he noticed Heathcliff's nice clothes.

"Look at you!" he said sneering[1]. "Who do you want to impress[2]? Get out or I'll pull your hair until it's longer than it is now!"

"It's long enough already," observed[3] Edgar Linton. He was standing at the sitting room door. "It hangs over his eyes like a horse's mane[4]!"

Edgar didn't say this to insult[5] Heathcliff but Heathcliff had a quick and violent[6] temper[7]. He suddenly picked up a pan of hot apple sauce[8] and threw the contents[9] in Edgar's face.

---

1 sneer [snɪr] (v.) 譏諷
2 impress [ɪmˋprɛs] (v.) 使印象深刻
3 observe [əbˋzɝv] (v.) 評論；説
4 mane [men] (n.) （馬、獅等的）鬃

5 insult [ɪnˋsʌlt] (v.) 侮辱
6 violent [ˋvaɪələnt] (a.) 猛烈的
7 temper [ˋtɛmpɚ] (n.) 脾氣
8 sauce [sɔs] (n.) 醬汁
9 content [ˋkɑntɛnt] (n.) 內容物

Edgar screamed. Hearing her brother's cries, Isabella, followed by Catherine, came running out. Hindley grabbed[1] Heathcliff by the arm, took him to his room and gave him a beating[2].

I didn't have much sympathy[3] for Edgar but I cleaned his face. His sister was crying and wanted to go home. Catherine was confused[4] and embarrassed[5] and didn't say anything.

Hindley came back and told the children to return to the sitting room and have their dinner. As soon as they saw the food on the table they forgot everything because they were hungry.

I looked at Catherine. Her eyes were dry as she cut her meat[6].

"What an insensitive[7] child," I thought. "She doesn't really care about Heathcliff."

I watched her lift the meat to her mouth and then suddenly her eyes filled with tears. To hide her emotion[8] she dropped her fork on the floor and bent[9] down to pick it up. So she wasn't as insensitive as I thought!

Some musicians[10] came to play for us in the evening. While everyone was listening to them, Catherine escaped[11] and climbed the stairs to Heathcliff's room. She called him but there was no answer so she crawled[12] along the roof and climbed into his room through a small window. Later they came downstairs to the kitchen together. I gave Heathcliff some supper but he didn't eat it.

"I don't care how long I have to wait, Nelly," he said, "but I'm going to take my revenge[13] on Hindley. I only hope he doesn't die first!"

"Heathcliff!" I said. "You should learn to forgive[14]."

"No! I must have satisfaction," he replied. "I'm going to think of a good way to take my revenge. If I think about that, I won't feel the pain."

---

1 grab [græb] (v.) 攫住
2 beating [ˈbitɪŋ] (n.) 打
3 sympathy [ˈsɪmpəθɪ] (n.) 同情
4 confused [kənˈfjuzd] (a.) 混亂的
5 embarrassed [ɪmˈbærəst] (a.) 尷尬的
6 meat [mit] (n.) 肉
7 insensitive [ɪnˈsɛnsətɪv] (a.) 無感覺的
8 emotion [ɪˈmoʃən] (n.) 情緒
9 bend [bɛnd] (v.) 彎身（動詞三態：bend; bent; bent）
10 musician [mjuˈzɪʃən] (n.) 樂師
11 escape [əˈskep] (v.) 逃跑
12 crawl [krɔl] (v.) 爬行
13 revenge [rɪˈvɛndʒ] (n.) 報仇
14 forgive [fəˈgɪv] (v.) 原諒（動詞三態：forgive; forgave; forgiven）

6. Catherine's Choice

(31) Nelly Dean continued her story:

The following summer, that's nearly twenty-three years ago now, Hindley and Frances' son, Hareton Earnshaw, was born. He was a lovely, healthy baby but very soon after his birth, Frances died and I was given the job of looking after him.

After his wife's death, Hindley changed. He didn't care about anything any more. He started drinking[1] a lot and gambling[2]. After a while, all the servants left because he treated[3] them so badly. He also treated Heathcliff very badly but the boy put up with[4] it. He seemed to enjoy watching Hindley gradually sinking[5] lower and lower.

No-one visited the house except for Edgar Linton. He occasionally[6] came to see Catherine. At fifteen she was the queen of the countryside! I didn't like her then. She was too arrogant[7] and headstrong[8].

Catherine now led a double life. She was polite[9] and behaved like a lady with the Lintons but at home with Heathcliff she was as wild as always.

One afternoon Catherine and Heathcliff were in the sitting room together when Edgar arrived. Heathcliff left immediately. I stayed because Hindley didn't want Catherine and Edgar to be left alone.

I put little Hareton on the floor and started to clean some plates.

"What are you doing there, Nelly?" Catherine said crossly[10].

"My work, Miss," I replied.

She came up behind me and whispered angrily, "Go away! Servants don't start cleaning in the room when guests arrive!"

And then, thinking that Edgar couldn't see her, she grabbed the cloth from my hand and pinched[11] me hard on the arm.

"Ouch[12]!" I shouted. "Why did you pinch me like that, Miss?"

"I didn't touch you!" she cried, her ears red with rage.

"What's that, then?" I said, showing her the red mark on my arm.

Furious, Catherine hit me on the cheek.

"Catherine, love! Catherine!" said Edgar, shocked at her violent behavior.

"Leave the room, Nelly!" she shouted.

Hareton was frightened and started crying.

She suddenly grabbed him and shook him hard. Edgar tried to pull the child away from her but she hit him too.

I took Hareton in my arms and went to the kitchen. Through the sitting room door, I saw Edgar pick up his hat.

---

1 drink [drɪŋk] (v.) 酗酒

2 gamble [ˈgæmbl̩] (v.) 賭博

3 treat [trit] (v.) 對待

4 put up with 忍受

5 sink [sɪŋk] (v.) 下沉（動詞三態：sink; sank, sunk; sunk, sunken）

6 occasionally [əˈkeʒənlɪ] (adv.) 偶爾

7 arrogant [ˈærəgənt] (a.) 傲慢的

8 headstrong [ˈhɛdˌstrɔŋ] (a.) 任性的

9 polite [pəˈlait] (a.) 禮貌的

10 crossly [ˈkrɔslɪ] (adv.) 乖戾地

11 pinch [pɪntʃ] (v.) 捏；擰

12 ouch [autʃ] (int.) 哎喲（突然疼痛時發出的聲音）

"Where are you going?" demanded Catherine. "You mustn't go!"

"I must and I will!" he replied quietly.

"No," she said, "not yet. Sit down. I'll be miserable[1] all night if you go home angry and I don't want to be miserable for you!"

"I'm ashamed of[2] you," he said. "I'm not going to come here again!" And he went to the door.

Catherine threw herself into a chair and burst into tears. Edgar was already outside but suddenly he turned round, hurried back into the sitting room and closed the door behind him.

Not long after that I heard Hindley's horse outside so I went to tell Catherine and Edgar. When I saw them I knew they were no longer just friends. They were now lovers.

Suddenly I heard Hindley entering the house. I went back to the kitchen to hide little Hareton from his father because the boy was terrified[3] of him. But it was too late. Hindley was staggering[4] through the door. He was drunk[5].

"I've found you at last!" he cried, and he picked up the little boy. "Now kiss me!" he shouted. "Kiss me or I'll break your neck!"

Poor Hareton was screaming.

I watched as Hindley carried him up the stairs. At the top he stopped, lifted the child over the banister[6] rail[7] and held him there.

---

1 miserable ['mɪzərəb!] (a.) 痛苦的
2 ashamed [ə'ʃemd] (a.) 羞愧的
3 terrified ['tɛrə,faɪd] (a.) 被嚇到的
4 stagger ['stægɚ] (v.) 搖搖晃晃

5 drunk [drʌŋk] (a.) 喝醉酒的
6 banister ['bænɪstɚ] (n.) 欄杆
　（尤指室內樓梯的欄杆）
7 rail [rel] (n.) 欄杆；扶手

"No!" I shouted and ran to rescue him. As I reached them, there was a noise below.

It was Heathcliff. Hindley looked at him and at that moment Hareton fell.

It happened so quickly that there was no time to feel shock. Fortunately Heathcliff managed to[1] catch him.

I ran downstairs and took the child from him. Hareton wasn't even crying.

Hindley came down slowly. He poured some brandy[2] into a glass and drank it all. Then he shouted: "Get out! All of you!"

Heathcliff followed me into the kitchen and opened the back door.

"I hope he kills himself with drink," he said going out.

I sat down.

"Are you alone, Nelly?" a voice said quietly. It was Catherine.

"Yes, Miss," I replied.

She came in and sat with me near the fire. She looked worried and I knew she wanted to tell me something. I continued singing to Hareton because I was still angry with her.

"Where's Heathcliff?" she said.

"Working in the barn."

But I was wrong. He was sitting outside the kitchen door. I didn't know that until later.

"Oh, dear! I'm very unhappy," she cried. "Nelly, can you keep a secret?"

"Maybe. It depends."

"Today, Edgar Linton asked me to marry him and I accepted."

"So, what are you unhappy about? Your brother will be pleased. The Lintons won't object[3]. Where's the problem?"

"Here! And here!" she shouted, hitting her head with one hand and her chest with the other. "In my soul and in my heart, I'm making a mistake! Edgar Linton isn't the right man for me. But I can't marry Heathcliff. Marrying him would only degrade[4] me. He has no money and no future now, thanks to Hindley."

THE RIGHT MAN?

- Imagine you are Catherine. Make notes on why Edgar Linton is and isn't the right man to marry. Do the same for Heathcliff.
- What will Catherine's life be like if she marries Edgar? And if she marries Heathcliff?

At that moment there was a movement[5] outside the door. I turned my head to look. It was Heathcliff. He was walking away. Catherine didn't notice him and continued talking.

1 manage to 設法
2 brandy [ˋbrændɪ] (n.) 白蘭地酒
3 object [əbˋdʒɛkt] (v.) 反對
4 degrade [dɪˋgred] (v.) 降低；降級
5 movement [ˋmuvmənt] (n.) 移動

"But, Nelly, if I marry Edgar, I'll have money. I'll be able to help Heathcliff to escape from my brother's power. Nelly, I am Heathcliff. He is always in my mind."

Just then Joseph came in and I had to start cooking the supper. When it was ready I went outside to tell Heathcliff to come in, but I couldn't find him. We didn't see him again for a very long time.

Nelly Dean finished the first part of her story.

7. Heathcliff's Return

The morning after my walk across the moor I woke up with a fever[1]. I was very ill and had to stay in bed for a month. I'm feeling better now but I'm still too weak to read. Bored with my own company, I have asked Mrs Dean to come up and tell me the end of my landlord's story.

She has brought her sewing and works as she talks to me.

Nelly Dean continued her story:

After Heathcliff left, Catherine caught a fever and was ill for a long time. The Lintons wanted to look after her so they took her to Thrushcross Grange. Unfortunately Mr and Mrs Linton caught the fever too and died within a few days of each other.

Catherine stayed at the Grange for several months and when she came back she was different. Her temper was worse and she treated me and the servants very unkindly sometimes.

Anyway three years later she and Edgar married. They asked me to leave Wuthering Heights and come here to the Grange with them. At first I said "no" because I didn't want to leave little Hareton. But Hindley didn't want me to stay so I had to leave.

Catherine was less bad-tempered after she came here, probably because she was allowed to do what she wanted.

I think Mr Linton was afraid of her temper and didn't want to upset her. When she was depressed[2] and quiet, he was quiet too. When she laughed, he laughed with her. They seemed happy.

HAPPINESS

- Do you think that Catherine and Edgar were happy?
- Describe a time you were happy. Who were you with? What were you doing?

But their happiness didn't last long. One September evening I was coming in from the garden with a basket of apples when I heard a voice behind me say, "Nelly, is that you?"

I turned round and saw a tall dark man standing behind me. "I've been waiting here for an hour."

He moved closer and I saw his eyes. It was Heathcliff.

"Is it really you?" I cried. "Have you come back?"

"I must speak to Catherine," he said. "Go and get her, Nelly! Tell her somebody from the village wants to speak to her."

Catherine and Edgar were sitting together in the parlor[3]. It was a peaceful scene and I didn't want to disturb them. However, I gave Catherine the message and she stood up and went downstairs.

---

1 fever [ˋfivɚ] (n.) 發燒
2 depressed [dɪˋprɛst] (a.) 感到沮喪的
3 parlor [ˋpɑrlɚ] (n.) 客廳

"Who is it?" Mr Linton asked me.

"That boy who lived at Mr Earnshaw's – Heathcliff," I replied.

"What! The gypsy?" he cried.

A few minutes later Catherine came running upstairs excitedly.

"Oh, Edgar, Edgar!" she cried as she rushed in. "Heathcliff's come back! Oh, I'm so happy! Shall I tell him to come up?"

Edgar's face was very serious.

"Catherine, calm down[1], please! There's no need to get so excited," he said. "He's only a runaway[2] servant. Nelly, go and tell him to come up."

Heathcliff was in the kitchen. By the light of the fire I could see him more clearly. He stood very straight, like a soldier. His face had an intelligent[3] expression and he looked proud and confident[4].

We went upstairs to the parlor. He chose a chair opposite Catherine and sat down. Her eyes were full of love as she looked at him. His, too, filled with love each time he looked at her. It was clear they were both really happy to be together again. Edgar saw this and it annoyed[5] him.

After an hour Heathcliff left. As he was leaving he told me that he was staying at Wuthering Heights.

I was shocked and afraid when I heard this.

That night Catherine came to my room. She wanted to talk about Heathcliff. She explained to me why he was staying at Wuthering Heights.

---

1 calm down 冷靜下來
2 runaway [ˈrʌnəˌwe] (a.) 逃走的
3 intelligent [ɪnˈtɛlədʒənt] (a.) 有才智的
4 confident [ˈkɑnfədənt] (a.) 有自信的
5 annoy [əˈnɔɪ] (v.) 使煩惱

"He wants to be near the Grange," she said, "so that we can see each other often. He's going to give my brother some money for a room. Hindley will agree. He needs money. He has a lot of debts[1]."

After that Heathcliff was a frequent[2] visitor at the Grange. Mr Linton wasn't very happy about the visits but he wanted Catherine to be happy. And she was. She was sweet and kind to everyone.

However, it soon became clear that Isabella was falling in love with[3] Heathcliff. She was eighteen and a very charming[4] young lady. She was sensitive[5] and intelligent but she was still a child. When she looked at Heathcliff she saw a handsome man with the manners[6] of a gentleman, nothing else.

Heathcliff didn't love Isabella, he only had eyes for Catherine. Edgar was worried. He was sure that Heathcliff was encouraging[7] his sister's feelings.

Then Isabella started to become visibly[8] unhappy. She stopped eating and became thin and pale. She was angry with everyone, especially Edgar and Catherine. Her brother didn't care about her, she said, and Catherine was unkind to her. This made Catherine angry.

"Why do you say that?" she demanded. "When have I been unkind to you?"

"Yesterday," sobbed Isabella. "When we were walking on the moor with Heathcliff. You told me to go away and walk somewhere else."

"I thought you were bored."

(41) "That's not true. You sent me away because you knew that I wanted to be with ..."

"Well?" said Catherine.

"With him! With Heathcliff! But you want to keep him for yourself! You don't want him to love anyone else."

"Isabella, do you mean that you want Heathcliff to love you?"

"I love Heathcliff more than you have ever loved Edgar. And he might love me if you let him!"

"You little fool! You don't know what he's like. Nelly, tell her about Heathcliff! Tell her that he is wild and fierce[9], like an animal. Tell her that there is no kindness in him. Tell her that he'll never love a Linton."

Isabella looked at Catherine angrily.

"I don't believe you. You say that because you're selfish[10]!"

"Alright. Do what you like! I don't care!" Catherine said and walked out of the room. Isabella burst into tears.

CATHERINE AND HEATHCLIFF

- What do you think? Is Catherine trying to protect Isabella or keep Heathcliff for herself?
- Why does she say that Heathcliff will never love a Linton?
- Why might Heathcliff want to marry Isabella?

---

1 debt [dɛt] (n.) 債務
2 frequent [ˈfrikwənt] (a.) 頻繁的
3 fall in love with somebody 愛上某人
4 charming [ˈtʃɑrmɪŋ] (a.) 有魅力的
5 sensitive [ˈsɛnsətɪv] (a.) 靈敏的

6 manners [ˈmænəz] (n.) 〔複〕禮貌
7 encourage [ɪnˈkɜɪdʒ] (v.) 助長
8 visibly [ˈvɪzəblɪ] (adv.) 明顯可見地
9 fierce [fɪrs] (a.) 兇猛的
10 selfish [ˈsɛlfɪʃ] (a.) 自私的

Catherine and Isabella were sitting in the library[1] when Heathcliff arrived the next day. They were still angry with each other and the atmosphere was tense. As soon as she saw him, Catherine jumped up and ran to greet him.

"Come in!" she said with a smile. "We're both happy to see you today. Heathcliff, here is someone who loves you more than I do. No, not Nelly! My little sister-in-law[2]!"

Isabella looked embarrassed and stood up to leave.

"No, no, Isabella, don't go away!" Catherine grabbed the girl's arm and held it tightly. "Yesterday we were quarreling about you, Heathcliff. Isabella says that she loves you much more than Edgar loves me."

Isabella's face turned white and then red. Her eyes filled with tears. She pulled her arm free and ran out of the room.

"Is that true?" asked Heathcliff.

"Yes," Catherine replied. "She's made herself ill because of you. But don't worry about her. I only wanted to punish her a little for being rude to me. I like her. I don't want you to hurt her."

"And I dislike her too much to try," Heathcliff said.

Then after a few minutes' silence, he asked: "She's her brother's heir[3], isn't she?"

"Not if I have children," replied Catherine. Then she added, "You think too much about your neighbor's property, Heathcliff! Remember this neighbor's property is mine."

1 library [ˈlaɪˌbrɛrɪ] (n.) 書房
2 sister-in-law [ˈsɪstəɪnˌlɔ] (n.) 小姑
3 heir [ɛr] (n.) 繼承人
4 traitor [ˈtretɚ] (n.) 叛徒

I decided to watch Heathcliff after that. I didn't trust him – or Catherine!

The next time Heathcliff came, Isabella was outside in the courtyard. I was standing near the kitchen window but they couldn't see me. He went up to her and said something. She looked embarrassed and tried to leave but he stopped her. Then, after looking quickly at the house, he put his arm around her and kissed her.

"Traitor[4]!" I cried.

"Who is, Nelly?" It was Catherine. She was standing behind me.

8. Heathcliff's Revenge

Nelly Dean continued her story:

Catherine looked out of the window and saw Heathcliff with Isabella.

When he opened the kitchen door and came in a few minutes later, she was waiting for him.

"I told you to leave her alone," she said. Although she was angry, she spoke calmly. "If you don't, I'll tell Edgar and you won't be allowed to visit again."

"If Isabella wants me to kiss her, why shouldn't I?" he replied. "I am not your husband. You don't need to be jealous[1] of me!"

"I'm not jealous of you," replied Catherine sharply[2]. "If you love Isabella, you can marry her."

"But what about Mr Linton?" I asked. "He won't let Heathcliff marry his sister."

"I don't need his permission[3]," Heathcliff growled. Then he looked at Catherine.

"You are a fool if you think I believe your sweet words, Catherine. You have treated me badly, but I'll take my revenge very soon. In the meantime, thank you for telling me your sister-in-law's secret. It has given me an idea."

They continued quarreling so I left them and went upstairs to look for Mr Linton.

"Nelly," he said, when I entered the library, "have you seen your mistress?"

"Yes, she's in the kitchen, sir," I answered. "She's with Heathcliff."

I told him about the scene in the courtyard and the argument between his wife and Heathcliff.

"I think you should do something, sir," I added.

He rushed downstairs and into the kitchen.

"Get out, Heathcliff!" he shouted at his visitor. "And don't come back! You aren't welcome here."

Edgar's angry words upset Catherine and she asked me to take her upstairs.

"My head aches[4] so much, Nelly!" she said. "Tell Edgar I'm ill. I don't want to see him."

But I didn't and a few minutes later he went to her room. I stood outside and listened.

"Are you going to continue seeing Heathcliff after today?" he asked calmly.

"I don't want to talk about it," she replied coldly.

"Do you want me or Heathcliff?" he asked. "You can't be his friend and mine. You must choose."

This was too much for[5] Catherine.

"Leave me alone!" she screamed. "Go away!"

She stayed in her room for the next few days and refused[6] to eat anything. On the third day I took her some toast. She ate it hungrily and then she asked: "Where's Edgar?"

---

1 jealous [ˈdʒɛləs] (a.) 吃醋的
2 sharply [ˈʃɑrplɪ] (adv.) 嚴厲地
3 permission [pəˈmɪʃən] (n.) 允許
4 ache [ek] (v.) 疼痛
5 be too much for somebody 對某人來說難以承受
6 refuse [rɪˈfjuz] (v.) 不肯

"He's in the library," I replied. "He's reading a lot these days."

She couldn't bear the idea that Edgar wasn't spending his time worrying about her. She was furious. Her rage quickly turned to madness[1] and she tore[2] her pillow with her teeth. Then she ordered me to open the window.

It was the middle of winter and a strong wind was blowing so I refused. She burst into tears and started to throw the feathers from her torn pillow around the room. I lost my patience[3] with her.

"Stop playing with those feathers!" I said sternly[4]. "Lie down! You need to rest."

As I went around the room picking up the feathers, she became quieter.

"I remember being in my bed at Wuthering Heights," she said in a dreamy[5] voice. "I remember the sound of the wind in the fir trees near the window. I want to feel the wind, Nelly! Just once more!"

I didn't want to upset her again so I opened the window. The cold wind rushed in and swirled[6] around the room. I closed it quickly. Catherine was lying on the bed, crying.

"How long have I been here?" she sobbed.

"Three days, miss," I replied.

"Open the window again, Nelly! And leave it open!"

"No, miss. You'll catch cold[7]."

"Then I'll open it myself."

---

1 madness [ˋmædnɪs] (n.) 精神錯亂
2 tear [tɛr] (v.) 撕碎 (動詞三態：tear; tore; torn)
3 patience [ˋpeʃəns] (n.) 耐心
4 sternly [ˋstɝnlɪ] (adv.) 嚴厲地
5 dreamy [ˋdrimɪ] (a.) 不清楚的
6 swirl [swɝl] (v.) 旋轉
7 catch cold 著涼

And before I could stop her, she jumped off the bed, opened the window and put her head outside.

I tried to pull her away but she was stronger than me. I was looking for something to put over her shoulders when suddenly Mr Linton came in.

"Oh, sir!" I cried. "My poor mistress is ill but she refuses to stay in bed. You must do something."

"Catherine ill?" he said. "Close the window, Nelly! Catherine?"

She turned and looked at him. He didn't recognize the tired, pale face in front of him and he stood there in shock for a moment. Then he took her in his arms and held her tightly[1].

"She needs to be quiet, sir. We must be careful not to make her angry again."

"I don't want your advice, Nelly," he said. "It's your fault that she's ill. You encouraged me to upset her. Why did you tell me about Heathcliff and Isabella?"

"I was only doing my duty[2] as a good servant," I said.

Suddenly Catherine screamed: "Yes! Nelly is my enemy[3]! She's a traitor! A witch[4]!"

She struggled[5] to escape from Mr Linton's arms. She wanted to hit me so I hurried out of the room.

"She needs a doctor," I thought.

I put on my cloak and set off for[6] the village.

As I crossed the garden, I saw something white. It was moving. I went up to it. Imagine my surprise when I discovered that it was Isabella's little dog!

It was hanging[7] from a tree in the garden with a rope[8] around its neck. It was nearly dead.

I took it down quickly and put it on its feet. In the distance[9] I heard horses' hooves[10]. It was a strange sound for two o'clock in the morning. I walked as fast as I could to the doctor's house.

WHAT NELLY SAW AND HEARD

- Who do you think wanted to hurt Isabella's dog? Why?
- Who was riding the horses that Nelly heard? Where were they going?

When I described Catherine's illness to the doctor, he decided to come and see her immediately.

"She hasn't eaten for three days," I said. "And she's behaving like a mad woman."

"I've heard that Heathcliff has returned," the doctor asked. "Is it true?"

"Yes. He visits the Grange frequently. But my master has told him to stop coming. He's worried about Isabella. He thinks she's in love with Heathcliff."

---

1 tightly [ˈtaɪtlɪ] (adv.) 緊緊地
2 duty [ˈdjutɪ] (n.) 責任
3 enemy [ˈɛnəmɪ] (n.) 敵人
4 witch [wɪtʃ] (n.) 女巫
5 struggle [ˈstrʌgl̩] (v.) 用力掙扎
6 set off for 出發前往某地

7 hang [hæŋ] (v.) 懸掛（動詞三態：hang; hung, hanged; hung, hanged）
8 rope [rop] (n.)
9 in the distance 在遠處
10 hoof [huf] (n.) 蹄（複數作 hooves）

"Isabella's a silly girl," said the doctor. "Mr Linton should watch her carefully. Somebody in the village saw her with Heathcliff tonight. They were walking in the fields behind the Grange. He heard Heathcliff ask her to run away with him."

The doctor's news frightened me. I remembered the sound of the horses' hooves. I ran home and went straight to Isabella's bedroom. It was empty! I didn't know what to do. Should I tell my master? It wasn't a good moment because he was anxious[1] about Catherine. I decided to say nothing.

Before the doctor went back to the village, he spoke to Mr Linton and myself.

"Mrs Linton's life isn't in danger[2]," he said. "She needs rest and quiet and she'll get better."

The next morning one of the maids[3] from the village told Mr Linton about Isabella and Heathcliff.

He didn't want to believe her at first but then he said, "Isabella went because she wanted to. Don't mention[4] her name to me again."

---

1 anxious [ˈæŋkʃəs] (a.) 掛念的
2 in danger 在危險中
3 maid [med] (n.) 女僕
4 mention [ˈmɛnʃən] (v.) 提及
5 completely [kəmˈplitlɪ] (adv.) 完全地
6 expect [ɪkˈspɛkt] (v.) 預期
7 disappearance [ˌdɪsəˈpɪrəns] (n.) 消失
8 devil [ˈdɛvl̩] (n.) 惡魔

Nelly Dean continued her story:

Catherine was ill for two months. During that time my master never left her side. When she finally began to get better, he was happy again. He was anxious for her to get completely[5] well again – not only because he loved her but also because she was expecting[6] a baby – his heir!

Six weeks after her disappearance[7], Isabella sent her brother a short note saying she was married. She was sorry for hurting him and she asked him to forgive her. He didn't answer it.

A few days later I received a letter from her. I have it here so I'll read it to you, Mr Lockwood.

Dear Nelly,

I know Catherine has been ill and I'd like to write to her but I can't. My brother hasn't replied to my letter so I'm writing to you. Please tell him that I love him and miss him.

I arrived at Wuthering Heights last night. Nelly, I want to ask you two questions. The first: how did you manage to live in this house and not become mad? No-one here has human feelings. The second: is Heathcliff a man or a devil[8]? What have I married, Nelly? I hate him. Please don't say anything about this at the Grange but come and visit me here soon.

Isabella

I told Mr Linton about the letter and he gave me permission to go.

Isabella and Heathcliff were both in the sitting room when I arrived. She was pale and her hair was untidy[1], but Heathcliff looked very well. I looked around. The room was very dirty – there was dust[2] everywhere.

Isabella was disappointed[3] that there was no letter for her from Edgar. Heathcliff immediately started asking me questions about Catherine.

"Mrs Linton is getting better," I said. "But her appearance has changed a lot and her character[4] is different, too. Mr Linton has only memories[5] now of the woman he fell in love with. He'll stay with her of course because he's her husband. It's his duty."

Heathcliff was trying to stay calm but he was obviously[6] very agitated[7].

"Before you leave this house, Nelly," he said, "you must promise to arrange[8] a meeting for me with her. I want to see her. I will see her! Do you understand?"

"You must not, and I won't help you!" I replied. "She has almost forgotten you now. Seeing you again will only upset her."

"Forgotten me! You know she hasn't, Nelly. She thinks about me much more often than she thinks about Edgar."

"Catherine and Edgar are very fond of each other," Isabella cried. "Don't talk about my brother like that!"

"Is he as fond of her as he is of you?" Heathcliff's voice was full of[9] scorn[10]. "Did he care when you left? Does he care about you now?"

"He doesn't know anything about my life now."

"I hanged her little dog before we left the Grange, Nelly," he said, "but my violence[11] didn't upset her. Now I have finally succeeded[12] in making her hate me."

He took Isabella's arm and pushed her out of the room.

"Go upstairs!" he shouted. "I want to speak to Nelly in private[13]."

He wanted to arrange a meeting with Catherine. I refused to help him fifty times, Mr Lockwood, but in the end I gave in[14].

"Let me know the next time Edgar goes away and I'll come," he said, giving me a letter for Catherine. "No-one else must be there, Nelly. Promise me!"

---

1 untidy [ʌnˈtaɪdɪ] (a.) 離亂的
2 dust [dʌst] (n.) 灰塵
3 disappointed [ˌdɪsəˈpɔɪntɪd] (a.) 失望的
4 character [ˈkærɪktə] (n.) 個性
5 memory [ˈmɛmərɪ] (n.) 回憶
6 obviously [ˈɑbvɪəslɪ] (adv.) 明顯地
7 agitated [ˈædʒəˌtetɪd] (a.) 激動的

8 arrange [əˈrendʒ] (v.) 安排
9 be full of 充滿
10 scorn [skɔrn] (n.) 輕蔑
11 violence [ˈvaɪələns] (n.) 暴力
12 succeed [səkˈsid] (v.) 成功
13 in private 私下
14 give in 退讓

I didn't give the letter to Mrs Linton immediately. I waited until Sunday when everyone else was at church.

It was a warm day. All the windows and doors were open to let in the fresh air. My mistress was sitting in the parlor. She was wearing a white dress and had a shawl[1] over her shoulders. Her face was very pale and her eyes had an empty, dreamy expression.

"I have a letter for you, Mrs Linton," I said gently. "You must read it immediately because it needs an answer. It is from Mr Heathcliff."

She looked worried and confused for a moment. Then she lifted the letter and read it. She sighed, pointed[2] to the signature[3] and looked at me.

"He's in the garden now," I said. "Shall I ask him to come in?"

But I didn't need to. The doors were open and the next minute he was striding[4] across the room. He took Catherine in his arms and held her and kissed her for a long time. He didn't look at her face – he couldn't. Like me, he knew that she was going to die soon.

"Oh, Catherine!" he cried. "Oh, my life!"

Then she pulled away[5] from him saying, "Heathcliff, you and Edgar have broken my heart! And now you both want me to feel sorry for you. I'm not going to. You have killed me but you are still healthy. How long are you going to live after I die?"

1 shawl [ʃɔl] (n.) 方形披巾
2 point [pɔɪnt] (v.) 指向
3 signature [ˈsɪgnətʃɚ] (n.) 簽名
4 stride [straɪd] (v.) 大步走（動詞三態：
   stride; strode; stridden）
5 pull away 離開

(54) Heathcliff's eyes were full of pain.

"Will you forget me? Will you be happy when I am in the earth?" she continued. "Will you say twenty years from now, "That's the grave[1] of Catherine Earnshaw. I loved her long ago"? Will you say that, Heathcliff?"

"Don't torture[2] me, Catherine!" he cried. "I'll never forget you."

"Oh, why can't we be together forever?" she said in a low voice.

He stood up and walked away. He didn't want her to see his face.

"Heathcliff!" she cried.

Although she was weak, she forced herself to stand up.

He turned round. His eyes were wet with tears. Suddenly she moved towards him, falling over. He jumped towards her and caught her, holding her tightly in his arms.

"Why did you leave me, Catherine?" he cried. "I have not broken your heart – you have broken it. And in breaking it, you have broken mine. What will my life be like without you?"

YOU HAVE BROKEN MY HEART

- The verb "break" goes with "heart" in this expression. Circle the correct verb in the following expressions.
  - Ⓐ leave/put your foot in it (say or do something embarrassing)
  - Ⓑ pull/push someone's leg (play a joke on someone)
  - Ⓒ give/take someone a hand (help someone)

"Stop! Stop!" sobbed Catherine. "If I've done wrong, I'm dying for it. It is enough! You left me too, but I forgive you."

Just then through the window I saw a group of people in the road. It was Mr Linton with the servants. They were coming back from church.

"The master is coming," I exclaimed. "You must go, Heathcliff! Quickly!"

Catherine was holding him very tightly. She didn't want him to leave her.

"I'll come again later," he told her. "I'll stay in the garden."

"No! Don't go!" she whispered, still holding him.

"Only for one hour."

"Not for one minute."

"I must. Edgar will be here soon."

"No! Oh, don't, don't go. Heathcliff, I'll die! I'll die!"

"Hush, hush, Catherine! I'll stay. If he shoots[3] me, I'll be happy to die beside you."

She fell against him and he picked her up in his arms.

"She's fainted[4], or she's dead," I thought.

When Edgar entered the room, his face went white. Heathcliff walked over to him and put Catherine's limp[5] body in his arms.

"Look after her," he said. "Then we'll speak."

About twelve o'clock that night Catherine's baby was born. We called her Catherine after[6] her mother. Two hours later her mother died.

---

1 grave [grev] (n.) 墓穴
2 torture [ˋtɔrtʃɚ] (v.) 折磨
3 shoot [ʃut] (v.) 射殺（動詞三態：shoot; shot; shot）
4 faint [fent] (v.) 昏厥
5 limp [lɪmp] (a.) 無力的；鬆軟的
6 call after 以某人的名字來命名

Nelly Dean continued her story:

The next morning at sunrise I went to look for Heathcliff. I had to tell him the terrible news and I wanted to do it as soon as possible. He was standing near a tree in the garden when I saw him.

He lifted his head and said, "I know".

He was in agony[1] and I felt sorry for him.

"How did...?"

He stopped. He couldn't say her name. Fighting his grief[2], he managed to ask at last, "How did she die?"

"Quietly," I replied. "Like a lamb[3]. Now she's at rest."

"No!" he cried. "you can't rest, Catherine Earnshaw! Not while I am still living! You say I killed you. Well, haunt[4] me! The murdered[5] often haunt their murderers. But stay with me always! I can't live without my soul!"

He threw back his head and howled[6] like an animal.

CATHERINE'S GHOST

- Is Catherine at rest? Or does her ghost haunt Heathcliff as he asks? Go back to the beginning of the story to check.

The weather changed the following Friday. A cold wind blew and it started to snow.

Mr Linton was asleep upstairs and I was in the parlor with the baby. Suddenly Isabella ran into the room. Her hair was wet and her clothes were muddy[7]. She wasn't wearing a coat or a hat, only a light dress and thin shoes. There was a cut[8] on her neck.

"I have run away from Wuthering Heights!" she said when she got her breath back. "Ask the servant to prepare the carriage[9] immediately, Nelly. I have to leave this place."

When she was satisfied that everything was ready for her departure[10], she agreed to take off her wet clothes and put on dry ones. Then I brought her a cup of hot tea.

---

1 agony [ˈægənɪ] (n.) 極度痛苦
2 grief [grif] (n.) 悲痛
3 lamb [læm] (n.) 小羊
4 haunt [hɔnt] (v.) 陰魂不散
5 the murdered 被謀殺的死者

6 howl [haʊl] (v.) 怒吼
7 muddy [ˈmʌdɪ] (a.) 泥濘的
8 cut [kʌt] (n.) 傷口
9 carriage [ˈkærɪdʒ] (n.) 馬車
10 departure [dɪˈpɑrtʃɚ] (n.) 離開

"I'd like to stay with you, Nelly," she said. "But Heathcliff won't let me. He's afraid that I might be happy here at the Grange. He wants us both to suffer[1]. I don't understand why Catherine loved him. He's a monster! But I'm not going to let him kill me."

She began to cry. Then she continued, "Heathcliff stays in his room all the time now. At night he goes out on the moor and returns early in the morning. When he came back from the moor yesterday, Hindley and I were in the parlor. The front door was locked so he couldn't get in. He started knocking on it and this made Hindley angry.

'He can wait for five minutes,' Hindley said. Then he stood up and took a knife out of his pocket.

'Sit there and don't say anything!' he said to me. 'I'm going to kill him. He's robbed[2] me, you and Hareton. He lent me a lot of money to play cards[3] but I lost all of it. Wuthering Heights is his now.'

Suddenly Heathcliff's face appeared at the window. His hair and clothes were covered in snow. His face was frightening. He hit the window violently[4] with his arm and broke it.

'Don't come in!' I cried. 'Hindley has a knife. He wants to kill you.'

But Hindley was already rushing towards the window. He tried to stab[5] Heathcliff in the neck but Heathcliff grabbed his arm. The knife turned and cut deep into Hindley's wrist. Blood immediately began pouring from the cut and Hindley fell on the floor.

---

1 suffer [ˈsʌfə] (v.) 受苦   4 violently [ˈvaɪələntlɪ] (adv.) 猛烈地
2 rob [rɑb] (v.) 搶劫   5 stab [stæb] (v.) 刺
3 play cards 打牌

Heathcliff jumped through the window, grabbed him by the shoulders and banged[1] his head on the stone floor several times. Then he suddenly stopped. Without saying anything, he tied a piece of cloth around Hindley's bleeding arm and left the room.

When I came down this morning, Hindley and Heathcliff were already in the kitchen. They both looked terrible. Seeing Heathcliff so weak made me feel stronger. I wanted to hurt him. I had to hurt him."

"That wasn't very nice, Miss," I said.

"He hurt me first, Nelly," she replied. "He'll never say he's sorry so I can never forgive him."

Isabella drank some tea and continued.

"I gave Hindley some water. 'Are you alright?' I asked him. 'He murdered your sister, and now he wants to murder you, too.'

Heathcliff heard me. He sighed and said, 'Go! Get out of my sight!'

There were tears on his face and all of a sudden I wasn't afraid of him any more.

'I loved Catherine, too,' I said. 'She was happy until you came back.'

That made him angry. He wanted to hit me but he was too far away. He picked up a knife instead and threw it at me. It hit me here below my ear. I pulled it out and threw it back at him.

He rushed across the room towards me but Hindley stopped him and they fell on the floor together. While they were fighting, I escaped and ran all the way here. But now I must go."

Isabella finished her tea and left for London without speaking to her brother.

She never came back but she wrote to Edgar regularly.

A few months after her escape she had a son. She named him Linton. He wasn't a very healthy child and he cried a lot, she said.

LINTON

- Why do you think Isabella calls her son Linton?
- What happens to Linton? If you can't remember, read the beginning of the story again.

Someone in the village gave Heathcliff her address in London but he didn't go to see her or the baby.

"I'll have the child one day," he said to me once. "When I want it."

Six months after Catherine's death, Hindley Earnshaw also died. He locked himself in the house one night and got very drunk. When Joseph broke the lock in the morning, he found Hindley on the floor dead. He was twenty-seven, the same age as me.

---

1 bang [bæŋ] (v.) 猛擊

I thought about the past, when he and Catherine and I were children. And I sat down and cried as if he were my brother.

I went to Wuthering Heights to organize his funeral. Heathcliff didn't try to stop me.

Just before we left for the church, Heathcliff picked Hareton up and put him on the table.

"Now you're mine!" he said quietly.

The little boy smiled at him but I was worried. I didn't trust Heathcliff.

"He must come back with me to the Grange," I said. "He's Mr Linton's nephew."

"Does he want him?"

"Of course he does."

"Well, tell him that if he has this boy, I'll make sure the other one takes his place[1]."

When my master heard this, he understood and never mentioned the subject of Hareton's future again.

Heathcliff was now the master of Wuthering Heights. Hindley left debts when he died so Hareton had nothing. He was a servant in his father's house.

THE OTHER ONE

- Who is the other boy that Heathcliff is referring to?

11. The Cousins

Nelly Dean continued her story:

The next twelve years were the happiest of my life. I looked after little Cathy, we called her Cathy not Catherine. And watched her grow up.

She was a lovely girl. She brought sunshine into our sad house. She had her mother's dark eyes, but the Lintons' fair skin and blonde[2] hair. She was gentle, not fierce and passionate like her mother. She was also an intelligent child and learnt quickly. She knew nothing about Heathcliff and Wuthering Heights because she was never allowed to leave the park.

Then one day a letter arrived from Isabella. She was dying and wanted to say goodbye to her brother. She also wanted him to take her son. Mr Linton prepared to leave for London immediately.

"Take great care of Cathy, Nelly," he said to me. "Make sure she stays inside the park. She mustn't go outside the gates, even with you."

It was summer time and Cathy played outside every day. She went for long walks and rode her pony around the park, but she always came back at teatime.

---

1 take one's place 取代某人的位置
2 blonde [blɑnd] (a.) 金髮的

(63) I didn't worry about her because I knew the gates were locked and she couldn't get out. One day, however, she didn't come back for tea so I went out to look for her.

"Have you seen our young lady?" I asked a farm worker. He was repairing a hole in the hedge[1].

"Yes," he replied. "This morning. She jumped over the hedge on her pony and galloped[2] away."

Imagine how I felt, Mr Lockwood! I squeezed[3] through the hole in the hedge and walked along the road for several miles but I didn't find her.

Then, as I was passing Wuthering Heights, I saw her dog. I ran up to the door and knocked loudly. A servant opened it.

"Are you looking for your little mistress?" she said. "Don't worry. She's here. Come in."

I went in and found Cathy in the sitting room. She was laughing and chatting[4] to Hareton. He was now a big, strong boy of eighteen. He was looking at her with astonishment[5].

"You are very naughty[6], Miss!" I exclaimed. "I won't allow you to play in the park alone again."

"Oh, Nelly!" she cried happily. "I have a lot to tell you. Have you ever been in this house?"

"Put your hat on and come home at once," I said.

"Is it your master's house?" she asked Hareton.

He looked down, swore[7] and turned away from her.

"Don't ask any more questions, Miss," I said softly. "Let's go."

1 hedge [hɛdʒ] (n.) 樹
2 gallop [ˈgæləp] (v.) (馬等的) 疾馳
3 squeeze [skwiz] (v.) 擠

4 chat [tʃæt] (v.) 聊天
5 astonishment [əˈstɑnɪʃmənt] (n.) 驚訝
6 naughty [ˈnɔtɪ] (a.) 頑皮的
7 swear [swɛr] (v.) 發誓 (動詞三態：swear; swore; sworn)

When we were ready to leave she turned to Hareton and said, "Bring me my pony! Hurry up!"

"I'm not your servant," the boy growled. "Don't tell me what to do!"

Now it was Cathy's turn to be astonished. At the Grange she was always treated like a princess.

"You wicked boy!" she said. "I'll tell my Papa about you."

"Don't be unkind to him, Miss," the housekeeper said to her. "Although he isn't the master's son, he's your cousin."

"My cousin!" cried Cathy. "But Papa has gone to fetch[1] my cousin from London. My cousin is a gentleman's son. This..."

She stopped and burst into tears.

"Hush!" I said. "You have more than one cousin, Miss Cathy. Come on. We're going home."

On our way back to the Grange I made her promise not to say anything to her father about her visit to Wuthering Heights.

A few days later we received a letter from Mr Linton. Isabella was dead and he was on his way home[2] with her son. Cathy was very excited about meeting her cousin from London.

"He's just six months younger than I am," she said. "How nice it will be to have someone to play with."

Linton was a pale, delicate[3] boy with a sad face. He was very tired after the journey from London and he wanted to rest.

He lay on the sofa in the library while Cathy stroked[4] his curls and kissed him. He liked this and smiled weakly at her.

(65)   Later that night Joseph, Heathcliff's servant, knocked on the door. He had a message[5] for Mr Linton.

"Heathcliff wants his son," the old man said. "I must take him back with me."

Edgar Linton was silent for a minute. Then he said in a calm voice, "Tell Mr Heathcliff that his son will come to Wuthering Heights tomorrow. He is in bed now and he is too tired to travel."

Joseph didn't want to leave without the child but Mr Linton pushed him firmly[6] out of the door.

"Heathcliff will come himself tomorrow!" the old man shouted. "I don't think you'll throw him out!"

My master looked worried.

"Nelly!" he said. "I want you to take the boy to Wuthering Heights on Cathy's pony early tomorrow morning. Don't tell Cathy where he is. Just say that his father wants to see him."

I did, and for the next few years the cousins grew up separately.

The weather was beautiful on Cathy's sixteenth birthday so she asked her father for permission to go for a walk on the moor.

We set off and walked in the direction of the Heights. Cathy ran ahead of me. She was looking for birds' nests[7] in the grass.

---

1 fetch [fɛtʃ] (v.) 去接過來
2 on one's way home 在回家的路上
3 delicate [ˈdɛləkət] (a.) 纖細的
4 stroke [strok] (v.) 用手輕撫

5 message [ˈmɛsɪdʒ] (n.) 消息
6 firmly [ˈfɝmlɪ] (adv.) 態度堅定地
7 nest [nɛst] (n.) 巢；窩

Then she disappeared for a moment and when I saw her again, she was talking to two people. One of them was Heathcliff; the other one was Hareton. The land on the Heights belonged to Heathcliff and we were trespassing[1]. I hurried towards them.

"I only wanted to see the eggs," she was saying. "But who are you?" she continued. "I know that man. Is he your son?"

"No, he isn't," Heathcliff replied. "But I have a son and you have met him. I live over there. Come and rest for a while before you return home."

"No, you mustn't," I whispered to Cathy.

"Be quiet, Nelly," said Heathcliff. "Hareton! Take the young lady home."

The young people started to run towards the house before I could say anything. Heathcliff and I followed them and as we walked he told me his plans for Linton and Cathy. He wanted them to fall in love and get married.

"And I'm going to make sure it happens," he said.

Linton was in the sitting room when we arrived. He was taller than Cathy now and he looked healthier. Cathy was delighted[2] to see him again.

"Now that I know you are here, I'm going to come and see you every day!" she told him.

"Your father won't like that," said Heathcliff. "He doesn't like me. We quarreled once."

---

1 trespass ['trɛspəs] (v.) 擅自進入
2 delighted [dɪ'laɪtɪd] (a.) 高興的

"Then Linton must come to the Grange," she replied.

"Oh, I can't walk four miles," the boy said. "It's too far for me."

Heathcliff looked at him with disgust[1].

"He's weak, Nelly. She'll soon see that. Hareton's different. He's strong. But she'll never look at him. He's a servant like I was. He's never had lessons so he can't read or write. But he isn't stupid. He suffers like I suffered."

Cathy enjoyed her visit to Wuthering Heights and the following day she spoke to her father about it.

"Why don't you want me to see Linton?" she asked. "Is it because you quarreled with Mr Heathcliff?"

"Heathcliff's a bad man, Cathy," her father replied. "When he hates people, he destroys their lives. I don't want you to go there again."

Cathy obeyed her father because she loved him. But she started to write to Linton secretly. They exchanged letters and little presents for several months. Then one day I found them in a drawer[2] in the library. The most recent letters were love letters.

"Linton didn't write these," I thought. "This is Heathcliff's work."

I threw them on the fire. When Cathy found out she cried and was sad for a long time.

---

1 disgust [dɪsˋgʌst] (n.) 厭惡
2 drawer [ˋdrɔɚ] (n.) 抽屜

12. The End of the Story

68

Nelly Dean continued her story:

That winter Mr Linton caught a bad cold and had to stay in bed for many months. Then I, too, was ill with a fever for three weeks. Cathy looked after us both – she was an angel! She spent all her days with her father or with me. We didn't need her in the evenings and I never asked myself how she spent them.

One evening, however, when I was feeling better, I went to her room to say goodnight to her but she wasn't there. I looked all over the house but I didn't find her.

"Perhaps she went for a walk in the park," I thought. So I went back to her room and waited for her. The moon was bright that night and there was some snow on the ground. Then I saw her. She was getting off her pony. A moment later she opened the door and came in.

"Miss Cathy!" I said. "Where have you been?"

"Oh, Nelly! You frightened me!" she exclaimed. "Don't be angry with me! I'll tell you the truth. I've been to Wuthering Heights. I've been every day since you and Papa became ill. Linton isn't well and he enjoys my visits so much. Don't stop me from going to see him, and please don't tell Papa about my visits."

"I'll think about it," I replied. "Now go to bed."

The next morning I told my master everything. He said that Cathy's secret visits to Wuthering Heights had to stop.

That was last winter. During the spring and the summer Edgar allowed Cathy and Linton to write to each other. Linton begged[1] her to visit him but Edgar didn't want her to go to the house again. Finally he agreed to a meeting on the heath[2] near Wuthering Heights.

"I can't go with Cathy, Nelly. I'm too ill," he said. "You must go. But stay on the heath!"

Linton was lying on the grass when we arrived. He was paler and thinner than before.

"Linton, you don't look well," Cathy said to him. "Why doesn't your father call the doctor?"

The boy didn't reply. He closed his eyes and his head fell on his chest.

"He's asleep," exclaimed Cathy impatiently[3]. "Nelly, he isn't interested in me any more. Why did he want us to meet?"

Suddenly the boy looked up and cried, "My father! He's coming!" He was terrified and tears ran down his face. "Don't leave me, Cathy! If you leave me, he'll kill me!"

I heard a sound behind me and turned round. It was Heathcliff.

"Get up, Linton!" he shouted. "And stop crying!"

1 beg [bɛg] (v.) 懇求
2 heath [hiθ] (n.) 荒原
3 impatiently [ɪmˋpeʃəntlɪ] (adv.) 沒耐性地
4 prisoner [ˋprɪznɚ] (n.) 囚犯

Linton was terrified. He tried to stand up but he was too weak and fell back on the ground.

"Cathy!" said Heathcliff. "Give him your arm and help him go back to the house!"

I told her not to but she didn't listen to me.

When we arrived Cathy went in with Linton, but I stayed outside. While I was waiting for her, Heathcliff suddenly pushed me into the room and locked the door. Cathy and I were prisoners[4]!

"Why has he locked us in?" asked Cathy. "What does he want from us?"

"Father wants us to get married tomorrow," said Linton. "He's afraid that I'm going to die soon. You'll have to spend the night here."

"Oh, poor Papa!" Cathy cried. "He'll be very worried about us."

Then Heathcliff returned. After sending Linton upstairs to bed, he locked the door again and went and stood next to the fire. Cathy went up to him.

"I'm not afraid of you!" exclaimed Cathy. "Give me the key! Let us go!"

Cathy reached forward and tried to take the key out of Heathcliff's hand.

"Don't touch me! And keep away from me or I'll hit you!" he shouted. "I hate you!"

His words shocked me but I knew I couldn't say anything.

At about nine o'clock he took us to a bedroom upstairs and locked the door.

Early the next morning he came and took Cathy away.

I was a prisoner at Wuthering Heights for five nights and four days. I saw no-one, only Hareton. He brought me some food once a day but never said anything.

On the fifth day Zillah, the housekeeper, unlocked the door and let me out. She was surprised to find me there.

"Everyone thought you were lost on the moor," she said.

I hurried down the stairs and found Linton in the sitting room.

"Where's Cathy?" I asked. "Has she gone?"

"She's upstairs," he replied. "She's locked in her room. She can't leave. Father says she must stay with us here. She's my wife now."

"Have you got the key to her room?"

"Yes, but it's upstairs and I'm too tired to get it now."

"Where is Heathcliff?"

"He's outside with the doctor. He says that my uncle is dying."

"Mr Linton! Dying!" I cried. "I must go back to the Grange immediately!"

I ran all the way. The servants were happy to see me again and hear that Cathy was safe. I went to see Mr Linton. He was in bed. His face was pale and sad. He looked at me and whispered her name.

"She's coming," I said.

I was getting ready to return to Wuthering Heights to rescue[1] her when Cathy herself ran through the door. She went straight to her father's bedside and she was with him when he died a few hours later.

Heathcliff allowed Cathy to stay at the Grange until after her father's funeral. Later that day, when we were sitting quietly in the library, she told me about her escape from Wuthering Heights.

"Linton felt sorry for me and unlocked the door," she said. "I climbed out of the sitting room window before it got light and ran all the way here."

Suddenly the door opened and Heathcliff walked in. Cathy stood up and tried to leave but he grabbed her arm.

"No more running away! You're coming home with me," he said.

"I'll go with you, Mr Heathcliff," she said bravely, "because Linton is the only person in the world I love. And I know he loves me. You love nobody and nobody loves you. I'm glad I'm not you."

Then she turned to me and whispered, "Goodbye, Nelly! Come and see me! Don't forget."

"I don't want you in my house, Nelly," Heathcliff said, pulling Cathy out of the door. "When I want to speak to you I'll come here."

I haven't seen them since that day but Zillah tells me what goes on there.

Linton's health got worse and he died.

After the funeral Cathy went to her room and stayed there. Heathcliff went to see her once to show her Linton's will². In it the boy left all his property and also Cathy's to his father so Thrushcross Grange is now his. Cathy has nothing."

DEATH

- Write a list of all the characters who have died in this tragic story and why.

Nelly Dean's story finished here.

---

1 rescue [ˈrɛskju] (v.) 營救
2 will [wɪl] (n.) 遺囑

A couple of weeks later I was feeling strong again. It was the middle of January. I didn't want to stay any longer in that cold, desolate[1] place so I moved back to London.

In September I had to return to Yorkshire so I decided to go and visit Nelly Dean at Thrushcross Grange. I knocked on the door and an old woman opened it.

"Mrs Dean doesn't live here any more," she told me. "She's at Wuthering Heights now."

As it was still early I walked across the moor to the farmhouse.

When I got there, I heard voices coming through an open window. I went up to it and looked in.

Cathy and Hareton were sitting at a table. There was a book in front of them and Hareton was reading aloud. He was wearing new clothes and looked very handsome. When he read a page correctly, Cathy gave him a kiss. It was clear the cousins were good friends now.

I went quietly to the back of the house and found Mrs Dean in the kitchen. She was surprised to see me.

"What are you doing at Wuthering Heights, Mrs Dean?" I said. "And where's Heathcliff?"

"Ah, so you haven't heard," she said. "He died."

"How long ago?"

"About three months ago. But sit down and I'll tell you about it."

---

1 desolate [ˈdɛslət] (a.) 荒涼的

(75) When I was sitting comfortably, she began: Zillah left
Wuthering Heights and Heathcliff asked me to go and be the
housekeeper. Cathy was happy. She began to spend more time
with me and Hareton in the sitting room. At first she made
fun of her cousin because he couldn't read or write. But they
gradually became friends. She started teaching him to read and
he helped her make a flower garden.

One evening when Heathcliff and I were alone he said, "Have
you noticed that they both have Catherine's eyes, Nelly? They
both remind me of her. Everything around me reminds[1] me that
she existed[2] once and I lost her."

Heathcliff's behavior became very strange after that. He went
out at night and didn't come back until the morning. He didn't
eat or drink anything. Sometimes he just sat and stared[3] in
front of him with a look of joy[4] on his face.

One morning as I was walking around the house, I noticed
that his bedroom window was open. It was raining hard so I
went up to close it. Heathcliff was lying on the bed. He was
dead. There was a smile on his face and one of his hands was
resting on the shelf near the open window.

People in the village say they have seen the ghosts of a man
and woman walking on the moors, Mr Lockwood. But I think
Catherine and Heathcliff are at peace now.

---

1 remind [rɪˋmaɪnd] (v.) 提醒   3 stare [stɛr] (v.) 凝視
2 exist [ɪgˋzɪst] (v.) 存在   4 joy [dʒɔɪ] (n.) 喜悅

A Personal Response

1 Answer the questions. Share your ideas with the rest of the class.

　a　Did you enjoy reading the story? Why/why not?

　b　In your opinion is Heathcliff a good character or a bad character? Explain your answer.

　c　Do you think that Catherine Earnshaw made the right choice when she married Edgar Linton? Why/why not?

　d　Which character did you like best?

　e　After reading the story, would you like to visit the moors of West Yorkshire?

　f　Imagine you are a film director. Which actors do you cast as Heathcliff and Edgar Linton? Which actresses as Catherine Earnshaw and Cathy Linton?

2 Work in small groups. Make a list of films or stories you know in which:

　a　the hero or heroine takes their revenge on someone.

　b　there is a tragic love affair.

　c　a ghost haunts a person or a place.

❸ Comprehension

3 How are these people connected to Heathcliff?

    ⓐ Old Mr Earnshaw

    ⓑ Mr Lockwood

    ⓒ Edgar Linton

    ⓓ Linton Heathcliff

4 How are these people connected to Catherine Earnshaw?

    ⓐ Nelly Dean

    ⓑ Isabella Linton

    ⓒ Cathy Linton

    ⓓ Hareton Earnshaw

5 Tick (✓) true (T) or false (F).

T F   a) Wuthering Heights was an appropriate name for Heathcliff's house.

T F   b) Mr Lockwood was warmly received when he went to visit Heathcliff.

T F   c) Nelly Dean was Catherine Earnshaw's cousin.

T F   d) Hindley Earnshaw came back to Wuthering Heights with a wife.

T F   e) Catherine didn't want to marry Heathcliff because he was poor.

T F   f) Edgar didn't try to stop Isabella from marrying Heathcliff.

T F   g) When Hindley died, Hareton inherited Wuthering Heights.

T F   h) Heathcliff wanted Hareton and Cathy Linton to marry.

6 Correct the false sentences in Exercise **5**.

7 Work with a partner. Try to remember how the things in the pictures below were involved in the story.

ⓒ Characters

8 Complete the sentences with the words in the box below.

> aunt   brother   cousin   nephew
> sister-in-law   son   uncle

a) Hindley is Catherine Earnshaw's ....
and Cathy Linton's ....

b) Linton Heathcliff is Edgar's ....
and Isabella's ....

c) Hareton is Cathy Linton's ....

d) Isabella is Cathy Linton's ....
and Catherine's ....

9 Work with a partner. Discuss the following questions.

a) What was Heathcliff like as a child?

b) What was Heathcliff like as an adult?

c) Did your feelings about him change during the story?

d) Is Heathcliff a monster or a victim? Give reasons.

10 Make a list of the differences between

a) Catherine Earnshaw and Isabella Linton.

b) Hareton and Linton Heathcliff.

11 Some of Brontë's characters have the same names.
What is the effect of this?

12 Think of a positive and a negative characteristic for each of the characters in the box and explain your choice.

> Catherine Earnshaw   Edgar Linton
> Hindley Earnshaw   Isabella Linton   Nelly Dean

For example	Nelly is kind because she cares about Hareton. She's not very patient because she gets angry with Catherine when she's ill.

13 Describe the feelings these family members have for each other.

- a Catherine and Hindley
- b Edgar and Isabella
- c Cathy and Linton

14 Which social class do the Earnshaws and the Lintons belong to? Tick (✓).

_____ a aristocracy

_____ b gentry (upper-middle class)

_____ c working class

15 Which social class does Heathcliff belong to at the following times in the story?

- a When Mr Earnshaw adopts him.
- b While Mr Earnshaw is alive.
- c After Mr Earnshaw dies.
- d When he returns from being away.

D Plot and Theme

16 Match the events (1-12) to the dates (a-l).

_____ a 1765
_____ b 1771
_____ c 1777 October
_____ d 1777 November
_____ e 1780
_____ f 1783
_____ g 1784 March
_____ h 1784 September
_____ i 1797
_____ j 1800
_____ k 1801
_____ l 1802

1 Cathy and Linton get married; Mr Lockwood visits Wuthering Heights.

2 Catherine dies soon after giving birth to a daughter.

3 Linton Heathcliff is born.

4 Heathcliff dies.

5 Catherine Earnshaw and Isabella Linton are born.

6 Edgar and Catherine get married.

7 Cathy Linton meets Heathcliff and Linton on her sixteenth birthday.

8 Mr Earnshaw dies; Hindley returns to Wuthering Heights with his wife Frances.

9 Mr Earnshaw brings Heathcliff to live at Wuthering Heights.

10 Catherine visits Thrushcross Grange for the first time and stays there for five weeks.

11 Heathcliff runs away from Wuthering Heights.

12 Nelly takes Linton to Wuthering Heights.

17 Describe the love that:

    ⓐ Heathcliff has for Catherine

    ⓑ Edgar has for Isabella

    ⓒ Linton has for Cathy

    ⓓ Edgar has for Catherine

18 There are many contrasting pairs of characters, places and themes in the story. Look at the examples below. Why do you think Emily Brontë included these pairs? Discuss each one with a partner.

ⓐ Houses	Wuthering Heights and Thrushcross Grange
ⓑ Loves in Catherine's life	Heathcliff and Edgar
ⓒ Sides of Catherine's character	wild and ladylike
ⓓ Two Catherines in the story	mother and daughter
ⓔ Generations of main characters	parents and children
ⓕ Families	the Earnshaws and the Lintons
ⓖ Narrators	Nelly and Mr Lockwood
ⓗ Main themes	love and revenge

19 How did Heathcliff get his revenge on the Earnshaws and on the Lintons?

20 Find places in the story where the weather and the landscape are described. Are they important to the scenes? Would the story be the same with a sunny landscape and climate?

E Language

21 Complete these sentences with the correct forms of the words in the box.

> allowed / allowing   comforted / comforting
>
> given / giving   left / leaving   locked / locking
>
> made / making   seen / seeing   stood / standing

a The floor of the sitting room at Wuthering Heights was .... of smooth, white stone.

b Lockwood tried to open the door to get in the house but it was ....

c Heathcliff and Catherine were .... each other by describing all the beautiful things in heaven.

d When Frances died, Nelly was .... the job of looking after Hareton.

e Hindley didn't want Catherine and Linton to be .... alone so he told Nelly to stay with them.

f Catherine was .... behind Nelly and she didn't see Heathcliff kiss Isabella.

g Isabella and Heathcliff were .... together in the village one night.

h Cathy was never .... to leave the park around Thrushcross Grange.

22 Circle the correct word.

a. Lockwood was boring/bored with his own company so he asked Nelly to tell him about Heathcliff.

b. Hareton was terrifying/terrified of Hindley so Nelly tried to hide the child from him.

c. Catherine's behavior was worrying/worried but Edgar didn't know what to do for her.

d. Nelly was shocking/shocked when she heard that Heathcliff was staying at Wuthering Heights.

23 Which prepositions do you use after the adjectives in the box? Write each adjective in the correct column.

afraid   cruel   curious   fond   worried   kind

of	about	to
a.	c.	e.
b.	d.	f.

24 Use suitable adjectives from Exercise **23** to complete the sentences.

a. The dogs were .... of Zillah and immediately went back to their corners.

b. Lockwood was .... about the life of his landlord.

c. When they were children, Catherine was very .... of Heathcliff.

d. Cathy was a sweet girl and .... to everyone.

TEST

🎧 76 **1** Listen and tick the correct picture.

a ☐

b ☐

c ☐

d ☐

P **2** Choose the correct answer, 1, 2, 3 or 4.

a Mr Lockwood had to stay overnight at Wuthering Heights because
1 it was too late to go back to Thrushcross Grange.
2 there were no servants to take him back.
3 he didn't feel well.
4 he hurt his back.

b Heathcliff ran away because
1 Catherine hurt his feelings.
2 he wanted to get away from Edgar.
3 Hindley treated him very badly.
4 he wanted to make his fortune.

c Isabella fell in love with Heathcliff because
1 he behaved and dressed like a gentleman.
2 he was kind to her.
3 she liked his wild passionate nature.
4 she wanted to leave Thrushcross Grange.

d Catherine became ill because
1 she saw Heathcliff kiss Isabella.
2 she couldn't live without Heathcliff.
3 she was expecting a baby.
4 she thought Nelly was a witch.

e Heathcliff wanted his son to marry Cathy because
1 he knew they loved each other.
2 he wanted her to live at Wuthering Heights.
3 he wanted to own Thrushcross Grange.
4 he thought she was lonely.

PROJECT WORK

Love in Wuthering Heights

Work in groups of four. Create a poster on the theme of love in *Wuthering Heights*. Consider the following.

a. Different types of love: passion; companionship; infatuation; romantic; brotherly.

b. Different characters who are in love: Hindley and Frances; Catherine and Heathcliff; Catherine and Edgar; Isabella and Heathcliff; Linton and Cathy; Cathy and Hareton.

c. Different influences on these types of love: passion; companionship; money; revenge.

d. Different ways the characters act in love: lose their identity; suffer; become cruel; are happy; have fun.

e. Different images you associate with each relationship: choose one of the following and look for more to illustrate your project or poster.

Present your project or poster to the rest of the class.

作者簡介　艾蜜莉‧勃朗特生於 1818 年 7 月 30 日，在家中六個小孩中排行第五。三歲時，母親過世，小孩們由一位姨媽帶大。他們住在西約克夏哈沃斯鄉下的一處牧師公館裡，父親在那裡擔任教區牧師。這個村落緊鄰一大片荒野，這裡的景色是艾蜜莉創作的靈感來源。

有一段短暫的時間，她和瑪麗亞、伊莉莎白和夏綠蒂三個姐姐一起去上學。 1825 年，瑪麗亞和伊莉莎白雙雙死於肺結核，夏綠蒂和艾蜜莉便被帶回家中。之後，她們和哥哥布恩韋的教育就由父親在教區裡負責指導。

艾蜜莉鍾愛哈沃斯一帶美麗多風的約克夏鄉村，她在遠離家鄉後，變得多病又憂鬱。 1837 年，她擔任過一陣子的私人教師。 1842 年，她和夏綠蒂一起去比利時的一家女子學院修學法文和德文。後來，她們兩姊妹在家鄉合開一間學校，但因學生不足而關閉。對大多數人來說，哈沃斯離大城鎮太遠了些。

艾蜜莉、夏綠蒂和妹妹安三人，都很喜歡寫作。 1846 年，三人共同出版了一本詩集。隔年，艾蜜莉的唯一一部小說《咆哮山莊》問世。 1848 年 12 月，艾蜜莉死於肺結核，長眠哈沃斯。

本書簡介　《咆哮山莊》是一則關於愛情與報復的故事，內容講的是一位有著吉普賽人外表的神祕人物希斯克里夫，從他童年到三十八歲辭世的一生。故事的場景設定在西約克夏的荒野地區，這是艾蜜莉‧勃朗特所熟悉和鍾愛的地方。這部作品，也是她唯一一部出版的小說。

小說的名稱，得自故事中兩座山莊中的一座，意謂著山莊座落在多風的山上。故事講述凱瑟琳‧恩蕭和希斯克里夫這對青梅竹馬之間未了結的愛，這份情感後來毀滅了他們自己，也摧毀了兩個家族。

故事透過兩個敘事者，用回溯敘述的方式講述出來。第一個敘事者洛克伍德先生，他向希斯克里夫租賃了畫眉山莊。第二個敘事者是納麗‧狄恩，她是一個女僕，向洛克伍德先生陳述前塵往生。這兩位敘事者都是故事中的在場人物，讓讀者可以透過第一手資料，同時獲悉過去與現在的現場情況。

這部小說的主題是愛情，以及未適當表達的愛情會如何傷害人們。這種未了結的愛足以轉愛為恨，因恨而報復。「自然」是故事中另一個重要的部分，自然與文明的衝突，呈現在希斯克里夫和情敵艾德加‧林頓的關係上。

《咆哮山莊》現在被列為英國的經典文學，然而這本小說剛出版時卻受到批評，認為它過於古怪、駭世，不過，卻一致都認為這本小說令人欲罷不能。

1. 咆哮山莊的訪客

P.13

我今天來見了房東希斯克里夫先生。在英格蘭這個美麗而多風的地方，我只有他這麼一個鄰居。

我到訪時，他就站在莊園的大門邊。他帶著狐疑的眼神，用他的黑色眸子打量我。

「您是希斯克里夫先生？」我說。

他點點頭。

「先生，我承租了您的畫眉山莊，我是洛克伍德先生。」

「進來！」他一邊打開大門，一邊冷冷地說道。

我不擅長交際，而我感到希斯克里夫先生比我更不善與人打交道。

我騎馬穿過大門，他跟在後面，沿著小徑走回屋子。我們進入院子後，他對一位老翁喊道：「喬瑟夫，把希斯克里夫先生的馬牽走，然後給我們帶些酒過來！」

希斯克里夫先生的宅第稱做「咆哮山莊」。「咆哮」在當地話來講，是暴風、多風的意思，把這個地方形容得很貼切，房子矗立山頭，有一面沒幾棵樹，而且每棵樹都被呼嘯的北風吹得倒向同一邊。

P.14

我們走進起居室，起居室的地板由平滑的白色石頭砌成，裡面有一個大壁爐，另一邊是一個大餐具櫥，在房間陰暗的角落裡，還躺著幾隻大型的獵狗。

這是一個陳設簡單而舒適的農家住屋，不過希斯克里夫先生跟這裡不太搭調，他看起來不像農夫。他身材高大，長相英俊，膚色黝黑，像吉普賽人，而且一身紳士的穿著。他臉上的表情很冷峻，甚至帶點殘酷。當然，我可能是錯的。

我在靠近爐火旁的一張椅子上坐下來，而他就站在我對面。這時有一隻母狗走向我，我伸出手摸牠，牠露出牙齒，對我嗥叫。

「你最好不要碰牠，牠不是寵物。」希斯克里夫先生咆哮道。

接著，他走過房間來到門邊，又對老僕喊了一次：「喬瑟夫！」

老僕還是沒有動靜，希斯克里夫先

生便走出房間去找人，留我一個人和狗獨處。我靜靜地坐著，盯著狗看了一會兒，突然，那隻母狗往我身上撲過來，我想把牠推開，未料其他的狗也跟著一起撲上來。

我大喊救命，這時，一個身材魁梧的婦人，拿著一把煎鍋，奔進房間裡來。她一邊對狗揮舞著煎鍋，一邊大吼。狗很怕她，都乖乖地溜回陰暗的角落裡。

P. 15

這時，希斯克里夫先生回到了房間。

「發生什麼事了？」他沒好氣地問。

「你的狗像獅子一樣，根本是野獸！讓牠們跟陌生人獨處，太危險了！」我說。

「牠們是獵狗。」他回答：「來，這杯酒給你！」

「免了！」我冷淡地說。

「別這樣，洛克伍德先生，別氣，喝點酒。我們這裡很少有訪客，我和我的狗都忘了待客之道。」

我盡量讓自己氣消，便開始攀談起來。沒想到的是，我們相談甚歡。

臨走時，我說：「我明日再來訪。」

他似乎不喜歡這個提議，但也沒有加以拒絕。

希斯克里夫先生

- 為什麼希斯克里夫先生的外表會讓洛克伍德先生感到驚訝？
- 你認為希斯克里夫先生可能過著什麼樣的生活？
- 你想，洛克伍德先生下次來訪時，可能會發生什麼事？

P. 16

隔天，我吃過午餐後便出發。今天天氣冷冽，天空灰濛濛的。我敲著咆哮山莊的大門，這時飄下了雪。

沒有人來應門。我繼續再敲門，搖著門閂。

喬瑟夫聽到了聲音，從馬房的門口鑽出來。

「主人在田裡。」他喊道。

「家裡沒有其他人嗎？」我說。

「只有夫人，不過她不會開門的。」他說完，就又走回馬房裡。

這時雪下得很大，我快凍僵了。我想進門，可是門鎖住了。

這時，庭院突然出現了一位年輕人，他跟我招手，要我跟他走。

我們繞到房子的後面，穿過廚房，進到了起居室。房間裡爐火熊熊，桌子上擺了杯盤，旁邊還坐了一個女孩。

「她想必就是這家的女主人了吧。」我想。

她用一副冷淡、漠不關心的態度打量我，不發一語，令我感到很不自在。

「坐下！他很快就回來。」年輕人說道，態度不是很友善。

P. 18

我這時清楚地看到了女孩的模樣，她年約十七，身材窈窕，長相清秀，一頭金髮披在肩上。她一雙眼睛很漂亮，但眼神中帶著不悅。

年輕人沒好氣地看著我，我看不出來他到底是不是僕人。他的穿著和講話的內容是像僕人沒錯。他一頭棕色的濃密

捲髮亂七八糟的，因為在戶外幹活，他的手和臉都被曬成褐色。不過，他的態度很隨便，帶著傲慢，沒有僕人的樣子。

他們兩個人都不搭理我，沒多久，希斯克里夫先生進了門，這讓我開心多了。

「先生，我來了，說話算數的！我可能要你在這裡待到雪停了，之後你的僕人或許可以帶我回去。」我說。

「他們都忙得很。」他回答，然後轉頭向年輕女孩說：「去備茶！」

女孩倒著茶時，我們把椅子拉到了桌子邊。

我們不發一語地喝著茶，房間裡的氣氛很緊繃。我想這也是我造成的，便想講講話熱絡一下。

「這一帶的鄉間景色真是美，只是偏僻了些。不過，你看起來在這裡過得挺幸福的，與令夫人和家人……」

「夫人？」希斯克里夫先生對著四周瞧了瞧，大聲喊道：「在哪裡？你是在講她的鬼魂嗎？」

P.19

我真蠢！那個女孩怎麼會是他的妻子呢？他們兩個人的年紀差那麼多，她應該是年輕人的妻子才對！

「希斯克里夫夫人是我的媳婦。」希斯克里夫看出我的心思，便說道，臉上還帶著憎恨的表情。

「啊，是啊！年輕人，你命好，娶到這樣一個嬌妻。」我說。

年輕人漲紅了臉，低眼瞅著盤子。

「先生，我是說，她是我的媳婦，她嫁的人是我兒子。」希斯克里夫先生說。

「那這個年輕人是……」

「不是我兒子。」

「我叫哈里登・恩蕭。」年輕人生氣地吼道。

氣氛開始變得讓我覺得很沉重，我對自己說，咆哮山莊我不會再來第三次了。

好一陣沉默之後，我問道：「你有僕人現在有空可以帶我回去嗎？」

「這裡只有希斯克里夫、哈里登、管家季拉、喬瑟夫和我。」女孩說。

「那我想我得待到明天早上再走了。」我回答。

「你如果要留下來，就和哈里登或喬瑟夫睡一張床。」希斯克里夫先生用粗魯的口氣說道。他雖然穿著紳士，但行為舉止一點也不紳士。

P.21

我對他們每一個人都感到生氣，便站起身來，從希斯克里夫身邊擠過去，奔出屋子，踏進黑漆漆的庭院裡。門口邊掛了一盞燈，我抓起燈，朝大門急急走去。

突然，有兩隻毛絨絨的怪物對著我的喉嚨撲過來，把我撂倒。牠們把我壓在地上，希斯克里夫和哈里登趕過來，這才把牠們驅走。

我嚇得開始流鼻血。季拉聽到聲音，也走了出來。她立刻用冰水沖我的脖子，然後把我拉進廚房裡。

我感到很虛弱，無法站立。希斯克里夫叫季拉幫我找張床，讓在這裡過夜。

洛克伍德
- 想像一下如果你是洛克伍德，你會作何感想？和夥伴分享看法。

2. 窗口邊的鬼魅

P. 22

季拉帶我樓上，來到一個房間裡。

「不要發出聲音！主人通常不准別人待在這個房間裡。」她說。

「為什麼？」我問。

「我不清楚。我來這裡才兩年。這房子裡怪事一大堆，我索性不問了。」她回答。

我關上門，爬到床上。我把燭火擱在一堆舊書旁的架子上，無意間看到架子上有字跡，漆面上刻劃著三個名字：凱瑟琳·恩蕭、凱瑟琳·希斯克里夫、凱瑟琳·林頓。

P. 23

我盯著這些字，直到眼皮開始下沉，昏昏欲睡。沒一會兒，黑暗中開始浮現出這些白色的字，我霎時醒了過來。

「我來翻一下書。」我心想，便從架子上抽出一本書。

這是一本日記，第一頁寫著「凱瑟琳·恩蕭的書」，日期是在二十五年前。我對凱瑟琳有點好奇，便讀了起來。

凱瑟琳
- 你想這三個凱瑟琳是誰？
- 凱瑟琳·恩蕭和哈里登·恩蕭，可能是什麼關係？

其中一頁日記，寫著咆哮山莊的某個星期天。我了解了一些來龍去脈：凱瑟琳·恩蕭的父親已經過世，她和個性殘暴的哥哥亨得利同住。

雖然我很睏，但我又讀了幾頁，脈絡逐漸清楚起來。凱瑟琳和希斯克里夫是很親密的朋友，而亨得利和他年輕的妻子法蘭絲很討厭希斯克里夫。

P. 24

之後，我把頭擱在枕頭上，又沉沉睡去。這一晚，我做了可怕的惡夢。我聽到有很多乒乒乓乓的聲音，便醒了過來。

窗外的樹枝，正敲打著玻璃窗。我翻

了個身，繼續睡，但夢裡還是持續聽到敲打聲。我決定把聲音止住。

我起身，把手穿過玻璃，將手臂探出窗外。然而，我的手指並沒有抓到樹枝，反而是被一隻冰冷的小手給攫住。那隻手緊緊揪住我，並且傳來一個哀怨的哭訴聲：「讓我進去！」

「你是誰？」我問。

「凱瑟琳・林頓！」聲音答道：「我回來了！我在荒野那邊迷了路！讓我進去！」

「我怎麼讓你進來呀？你要先把我的手放開，我才有辦法讓你進來啊！」我說。

手指鬆開了，我將手從窗外縮回來，然後拿了一些書擋在破掉的玻璃窗前。

我傾耳聽，聲音繼續哀叫道：「讓我進去！」

「走開！」我大喊道。

窗外那隻手用手指抓著玻璃窗，我想起身，卻動彈不得。我又嚇得大聲叫喊。接著，我聽到房門外有腳步聲，有人把門推開了。

「是誰在裡頭？」聲音說道。

P. 26

我坐起來，全身打著哆嗦，直冒冷汗。是希斯克里夫，他穿著襯衫和長褲，手裡拿著蠟燭，站在門邊。他的臉色和他身後的牆面一樣蒼白。

「先生，就我，洛克伍德。」我大喊出來：「我做了個可怕的惡夢，在夢裡大叫，很抱歉吵到你。」

「你怎麼會睡在這間房間？是誰帶你進來的？說！」他氣呼呼地說。

「是你的女僕季拉。」我答道。我爬下床，開始換衣服，「她大概是想證明這屋子裡有鬼，對，沒錯！整個屋子裡都是鬼！」

「你在說什麼？」希斯克里夫說：「你在做什麼？回到床上，不要再發出那種鬼聲音了。」

「我要去院子裡走走，等天亮，然後我就回家。而且，你不用擔心了，我不會再來了！」我說。

「隨便你要去哪裡，把蠟燭帶上，我等一下去找你。」他喃喃說道。

我走出房間，楞在門口，不知道要走哪一邊出去。

希斯克里夫沒有注意到我還在門口，他爬上床，把窗戶打開，然後突然哭了起來。

「進來！快進來！」他哽咽道：「凱瑟琳，快進來！噢，心愛的！」

P.27

凱瑟琳

• 你想希斯克里夫對凱瑟琳是什麼樣的感情？

我不想讓希斯克里夫覺得尷尬，便逕自下樓。

我在廚房裡等到天微亮，然後逃進清晨的冷空氣中。

在我穿越花園時，我的房東喊住我，說要帶我穿過荒野。我很高興他要帶我，因為雪茫茫的大地就像一片白色的大海，根本看不到路。

我們朝畫眉山莊前進，一路上沒說什麼話。他送我到林園的門口後，就掉頭離開。從這裡走回屋子不過兩哩遠，我卻迷了幾次路。等我回到屋子裡時，剛好在敲十二點的鐘響。

我的管家狄恩太太看到我很是高興。

「我們好擔心啊，下大雪時很容易在荒野上走丟。」她說。

我換了套衣服，走下書房。書房裡的壁爐燒著明亮的火焰，桌上還擺著熱咖啡。我在我的扶椅上坐下來，經過不得安寧的夜晚，又穿越荒野走了這麼遠的路，我覺得很虛弱、很疲憊。

3. 恩蕭家

P.28

我之所以搬來畫眉山莊，是因為想獨處，不想跟人講話。然而，在書房待沒

幾個鐘頭後，我開始覺得憂鬱、孤獨。於是，當狄恩太太送晚餐進來時，我請她留下來和我講講話。她答應了，便去拿她的針線活過來。

等她坐定之後，我說：「狄恩太太，你在這裡住了很久了，對吧？十六年了有吧？」

「先生，是十八年了，夫人結婚時我就來了。她過世之後，主人要我留下來當管家。」

她這時停頓了一下。

「唉，夫人過世後，世道也變了。」

「是啊，我猜也是。」我說。

我很好奇咆哮山莊那些人到底是怎麼一回事，我想狄恩太太一定知道吧，便決定扯到這個話題上。

「希斯克里夫為什麼住咆哮山莊，而不住畫眉山莊？畫眉山莊住起來舒適多了，難道他不是太寬裕嗎？」我問。

「先生，他很有錢，要住比這個更好的房子都不成問題，只是他不愛花錢。這很奇怪，他又沒家人。」

「他不是有一個兒子嗎？」

P. 29

「他是有一個兒子，不過去世了。」

「那個年輕的小姐，希斯克里夫夫人，不是他兒子的遺孀嗎？」

「是啊。」

「她是從哪裡嫁過來的？」

「先生，她是從畫眉山莊嫁過去的。她是我以前的主人林頓先生的女兒，她在嫁過去之前叫做凱瑟琳·林頓。」

「什麼？凱瑟琳·林頓？」我驚叫了起來。（但是不可能，她不可能就是昨晚那個女鬼。）

「你以前的主人叫做林頓？」我繼續問。

「是的，先生。」她答道，接著放下手上的針線活，問道：「凱希還好嗎？」

「你是說希斯克里夫夫人嗎？她看起來很好，只是不是很開心的樣子。」

「哎，這我倒不覺得奇怪。那你覺得山莊的主人，人怎麼樣？」

「他脾氣很硬，而且滿粗魯的，狄恩太太。」

「他是這樣沒錯。」

「你知道他的過去嗎？」

P. 30

「他的事我知道得可多了，不過我不知道他的父母親，也不知道他是怎麼發大財的。」

「那個男孩恩蕭又是誰？」

「哈里登·恩蕭是少夫人的表哥，少夫人和小主人也是表姊弟，一個是媽媽那邊的表哥，一個是爸爸那邊的表弟。希斯克里夫娶了林頓先生的妹妹，你看，

可憐的哈里登，他不知道希斯克里夫耍詐，霸佔了他的財產。」

「狄恩太太，請再跟我多說一點這位鄰居的事情，不然我會睡不著覺，拜託。」

她似乎樂於奉命，開始滔滔說了起來。

納麗·狄恩陳述的故事：

我來這裡之前，在咆哮山莊待過很長的時間。我媽媽負責照顧亨得利·恩蕭，他是哈里登的父親。亨得利和我同年，他的妹妹凱瑟琳比我們小八歲。

有一天，恩蕭先生出門去利物浦作生意，三天後他回來時，身邊多了一個男孩。男孩年紀不大，跟凱瑟琳差不多。他衣衫襤褸，全身髒兮兮的，看起來很像吉普賽人。他們叫他「希斯克里夫」。

沒過多久，恩蕭先生去世了，留下三個也沒了媽媽的小孩。

P. 31

兄弟姊妹
• 和夥伴討論有兄弟姊妹的優點和缺點，然後寫下來，和其他同學分享你的看法，並做比較。
• 有兄弟姊妹比較好，還是當獨生子女比較好？大家可以票選一下。

凱瑟琳和希斯克里夫成了很親密的朋友，不過亨得利一直很討厭希斯克里夫。我得說，我也不太喜歡希斯克里夫。希斯克里夫是一個奇怪的小孩，亨得利打他時，他都不會叫，也不會哭。恩蕭老主人發現兒子會欺負希斯克里夫時，非常火大。顯然地，希斯克里夫最

得他的緣。

我常常納悶為什麼恩蕭先生會那麼喜歡他，希斯克里夫從來不會對老先生表現出任何情感，或是做出什麼表達感恩之情的動作。但老先生的偏心，倒成了他對付亨得利的靠山。

我記得有一次，恩蕭先生買了一對小馬，給兩個男孩一人一匹。希斯克里夫挑了比較漂亮的那匹，但他的馬後來傷到了腳，他就想和亨得利換馬。

P. 33

「把你的馬給我，我不喜歡我的馬，如果你不跟我換，我就跟你爸告狀，說你是怎麼打我的。」

亨得利拾起一根鐵棒，說道：「滾遠一點！」

「你丟啊！」希斯克里夫沒有走開，他回嘴道：「我還要跟他說，等他一死，你就會把我趕走。」

亨得利將鐵棒一擲，砸到了希斯克里夫的胸口，讓他跌到了地上，不過他很快又站了起來。他臉色蒼白，冷靜地瞪著亨得利。

「你要就給你，吉普賽人！你最好被馬踢到！」亨得利大喊道。

當希斯克里夫從馬的背後走過準備換馬鞍時，亨得利突然推了他一下，讓他跌到馬腳下，然後自己拔腿跑掉。

希斯克里夫什麼話都沒說，他站起身來挺住，讓胸口緩緩氣。

之後，他進到屋子裡時，沒有讓恩蕭先生看他胸口上的傷。我原本還以為他不是一個會懷恨的小孩，但我錯了，這你以後就會知道。

4. 林頓家

P. 35

納麗狄恩繼續說著：

恩蕭先生年紀大了，身體愈來愈不行，脾氣變得很大。亨得利常會說話欺負希斯克里夫，讓他很生氣。有一、兩次，老先生氣得想拿拐杖打兒子，但他根本沒有力氣，只能氣得發抖。

最後，副牧師勸他送亨得利去學校。恩蕭先生同意了，不過看到兒子要離開，他很難過，但我可不難過。

「這下終於可以天下太平了吧。」我想。

凱瑟琳仍留在家裡。她是小美人兒，有一頭濃密的黑色捲髮，一雙黑色的眸子。她的個性很熱情，從早上起床到晚上上床，不是在講話，就是在唱歌，再不就是在笑。她喜歡扮家家酒扮演女主人，對亨得利啊、希斯克里夫啊、我啊發號施令。兩個男生要是不聽她的指令，她就會對他們動手動腳。不過，我可是不讓她打我的喲。

他很喜歡希斯克里夫，喜歡得過頭囉。對於凱瑟琳，我們想得出來最狠的懲罰方法，就是把他們兩個人分開。

P. 36

不久，在十月的一個夜晚，恩蕭先生坐在自己的椅子上，靜靜地離開人世了。凱瑟琳和希斯克里夫都很難過，一直哭、一直哭，但我得趕緊去村子裡找醫生，沒有空安慰他們。

等我回來之後，隨即去到他們的房間。那時已經過了半夜十二點，他們還沒睡。他們對彼此說著天堂裡是如何的美好，藉以互相安慰。我聽著聽著，不禁潸然淚下。

亨得利趕回家奔喪，結果身邊多了個妻子！我們大家都嚇了一跳。他的妻子很年輕、很漂亮，非常的瘦，一雙眼睛像鑽石一樣閃亮亮的。她的名字叫做法蘭絲，她在葬禮上不斷地顫抖，哭哭啼啼的。她跟我們說，她很害怕死亡。後來，我發現她在上下樓梯時，呼吸會有點不順暢。

一開始，法蘭絲很高興多了一個新妹妹，不過她對凱瑟琳的熱情沒有維持太久。至於希斯克里夫，完全不得她的緣。她不喜歡希斯克里夫進起居室，亨得利便要他去廚房和僕人待在一塊。亨得利還叫副牧師不要再來幫他上課，要他去田裡和那些農村男孩一起幹活。

剛開始，希斯克里夫還無所謂，反正凱瑟琳會把自己上課所學的東西教給他，而且還會和他一起在田裡工作或嬉戲。他們沒人照顧，就像野小孩一樣自己長大。

P. 38

他們很喜歡在荒野那邊奔跑，有時候會一早就出去，在那裡待上一整天——這可是他們受到的處罰，但他們無所謂，只要兩人能在一起，他們就什麼都忘了。

懲罰

- 凱瑟琳和希斯克里夫被處罰要去荒野待著，而你們的學校會用什麼方式來管教學生？你覺得這種管教方式有用嗎？
- 你有被處罰過嗎？是為了什麼原因？分成四人小組來討論，分享彼此的看法。

一個星期天晚上，他們因為發出了一點噪音，被趕出起居室。當我走去叫他們吃飯時，卻怎麼也找不到人。我們找遍整個房子，樓上樓下和庭院都不見人影。亨得利因此大發雷霆。

「把門鎖上，他們要是回來了，不准他們進門！」他說。

大家都上床睡覺了，但我很擔心，根本睡不著。我打開窗戶，想聽聽看有沒有他們的聲音。沒多久，我聽到了腳步聲。我看到路上有人提著一盞燈，那是希斯克里夫，他單獨一個人，我趕緊跑下樓打開門。

P. 39

「凱瑟琳小姐呢？她出事了是不是？」我叫道。

「她在畫眉山莊，但他們不要我留在那裡，所以我就回來了。」他回答說。

「哎，你們現在麻煩大了！」我說：「你們去畫眉山莊做什麼去了？」

「納麗，我先把外套脫掉，再跟你說是怎麼回事。」他回答。

他一邊換衣服，一邊跟我說了原委。

「凱瑟琳和我在荒野散步時，我們看到了畫眉山莊的燈光，便想去看一下窗戶裡面的情況。

我們跑下山，躲在起居室的窗戶外面，裡頭的燈是亮著的，我們看到——哇！裡頭真漂亮，納麗！好華麗的地方！有紅色的地毯，椅上和桌子都有紅色的布套著，純白的天花板鑲著金邊，中間吊著一個有玻璃墜子和銀鍊子的燈。

房間裡只有艾德加和她的妹妹，你猜他們在做什麼？伊莎貝拉，我猜她十一歲吧，比凱瑟琳小一歲，她躺在房間的另一頭，在那邊尖聲大叫。而艾德加站在這一邊的壁爐旁，靜靜地流著眼淚。桌子中間坐了一隻小狗，他們正在為那隻狗吵架。

P. 41

真是白痴！我們看得不禁大笑，結果被他們聽到了。他們嚇得開始大叫：『媽！爸！』

這時有人打開前門，我們於是拔腿就跑。我抓起凱瑟琳的手，但凱瑟琳突然摔倒。

『你快跑，希斯克里夫，快跑！』她小聲說道：『他們放狗出來，我被咬住了！』

狗的嘴咬住她的腳踝，納麗，她沒有哭啊。後來，一位僕人拿著一盞燈趕過來，把狗驅走，救起凱瑟琳。凱瑟琳的腳很痛，僕人把她抱進屋子，我尾隨在後。

『怎麼回事？』林頓先生問。

『先生，我們抓到這個小女孩，還有一個小男孩。』僕人說。

林頓先生把我拉到華麗的吊燈下，那兩個小孩也走了過來。

『爸爸，他好可怕喔！把他關進地下室。』伊莎貝拉說。

艾德加望著凱瑟琳。

『是恩蕭小姐，我在教堂看過她。』他小聲對母親說：『你看她的腳，流血了！』

『恩蕭小姐？怎麼可能！』林頓夫人叫道，然後再仔細端詳凱瑟琳，說道：『艾德加，你說的沒錯，是恩蕭小姐沒錯！』

她驚呼道：『她怎麼會和一個吉普賽人在荒野上跑來跑去？』

P. 43

『他不是吉普賽人，恩蕭先生在利物浦看到他，把他帶了回來。』她先生說道。

『他搞不好是一個壞孩子，我不要讓他待在我的房子裡。羅伯特，把他帶出去！』夫人說道。

我不想留下凱瑟琳自己一個人離開，可是僕人把我推進花園，要我走回家。納麗，我只好把她留在那裡了。」

5. 希斯克里夫的情敵

P. 44

狄恩‧納麗繼續說道：

凱瑟琳在畫眉山莊待了五個星期，一直待到耶誕節。當她返家時，已經不再是一個野孩子——她變成一位淑女囉。她棕色的頭髮上帶著一頂插著根羽毛的帽子，捲捲的頭髮柔順地披在肩膀上。

亨得利看到她時，驚呼道：「凱瑟琳，你看起來真美！比伊莎貝拉都漂亮了，對不對，法蘭絲？」

我幫她脫下外套，外套下是一件漂亮的絲質洋裝。她要狗別靠近她，生怕衣服會被弄髒。

「希斯克里夫呢？」她問道。

他躲在角落裡，眼前這個年輕的美人兒可嚇到他了。他知道這個人看起來不像凱瑟琳了。凱瑟琳一看到他，便跑過去抱住他，連親了六、七下，然後停下來放聲大笑。

「你怎麼滿臉不高興的樣子，看起來好怪、好兇喔！希斯克里夫，你忘記我是誰了嗎？」

「來吧，希斯克里夫，握個手嘛！」亨得利說完，便哈哈大笑起來。

「我才不要，你們在取笑我！」男孩說罷便要轉身離開，但凱瑟琳拉住了他的手臂。

P. 45

「我沒有取笑你的意思，只是你看起來很怪，而且髒兮兮的！」她說。

「我想髒就髒，我就是喜歡髒！」希斯

克里夫説完後，就快步走出房間。

當晚稍晚，我坐在廚房裡，想起恩蕭老先生對希斯克里夫的疼愛，我記得他老是擔心這孩子的未來。一想到希斯克里夫現在的處境，我不禁流下了眼淚。

「我一定要幫幫他。」我對自己説。我去院子裡找他，他當時正在馬廄裡幫凱瑟琳的小馬刷毛。

「希斯克里夫，快來！」我説：「來換上帥氣的衣服，我幫你穿，等凱瑟琳小姐下來時，你們可以一起坐下來聊天，聊到上床時間都可以。」

他繼續幫小馬刷毛，沒有理會我，我於是走回屋子裡。

隨後，他進了屋子，逕自走回自己的房間。

隔天，他早早就起床，出門去了荒野。

這時，其他家人去教會還沒回來，等他從荒野回來時，心情看起來好多了。

「納麗，讓我看起來體面些吧，我想變得好一點。」他説。

「希斯克里夫，聽你這麼説我真高興。你讓凱瑟琳很傷心，她大概很後悔這次幹嘛回家吧。」

「她説她很傷心嗎？」他用嚴肅的神情問道。

P.46

「我今天早上跟她説你不在時，她哭了出來。」

「我昨天夜裡也哭了，我才是應該要哭的人。」他回答。

「是沒錯，你什麼晚餐都沒吃就跑去睡覺！」我説：「你快去梳洗吧，把自己弄乾淨了，穿上最好的衣服，你看起來就會比艾德加・林頓帥氣了。」

他一邊穿上乾淨的衣服，一邊對我説：「納麗，艾德加・林頓的髮色比我淡，皮膚比我白，我很黑，他的穿著和舉止看起來都會比我好，而且他有一天會變成有錢人，而我不會！」

「希斯克里夫，你比他高，比他壯，比他勇敢。他很軟弱，怕東怕西的。」我回答：「你看看鏡子裡的自己！你不覺得自己很帥嗎？説不定你爸爸是中國的皇帝，你媽媽是印度的皇后！他們可能有錢到可以把咆哮山莊和畫眉山莊都買下來！你可能是被水手綁架來英國的，你就這樣想，這樣你就會覺得自己也很不錯，不會去計較亨得利欺負你了。」

比較一下你自己和別人

- 比較一下你自己和你所認識的其他人，並寫下來。例如：
  - 我比我兄弟高。
  - 我的數學比朋友湯姆來得好。
  - 我的眼睛比表妹瑪麗亞的眼睛漂亮。

這時，我們聽到院子裡傳來了馬車的聲音。希斯克里夫走到窗戶邊看，我則趕下樓去開門。

是林頓兩兄妹、亨得利、法蘭絲和凱瑟琳，他們一股腦兒跑進屋子，擠到起居室的大壁爐前取暖。

我叫希斯克里夫來加入他們。

希斯克里夫打開廚房的門時，亨得利正從起居室走出來。亨得利一看到他，就把他推回廚房裡，説道：「喬瑟夫，不要讓他進起居室！」

接著，他注意到希斯克里夫一身體面的穿著。

「看看你，你是想穿給誰看？出去，不然我就把你的頭髮扯得更長！」他不屑地説。

「他的頭髮已經夠長了，」站在起居室門口的艾德加・林頓評論道：「頭髮都蓋到眼睛了，像馬鬃一樣！」

艾德加並非有意要説話刺激希斯克里夫，但希斯克里夫瞬間被激怒，他突然拿起一鍋熱蘋果醬，往艾德加的臉上潑過去。

艾德加一聲尖叫，伊莎貝拉聽到哥哥的叫聲，連忙和凱瑟琳跑出來。亨得利扭住希斯克里夫的手臂，把他拉進他的房間裡痛揍一頓。

我不是太同情艾德加，但我還是幫他把臉擦乾淨。他妹妹哭哭啼啼，鬧著要回家，凱瑟琳默不作聲，不知如何收拾這種窘境。

亨得利回來時，叫孩子們回到起居室吃晚餐。他們已經飢腸轆轆，一看到桌子上的食物，便什麼都拋到腦後了。

我看著凱瑟琳，她切著肉，眼裡沒有淚光。

「好一個沒心肝的孩子，對希斯克里夫這樣無動於衷。」我心想。

我看著她把肉送到嘴邊，然後眼裡突然充滿淚水。她把叉子扔到地上，然後彎下身去撿拾，不讓人看到她的情緒。這樣説來，她並不像我想的那樣沒心肝了！

夜晚時，有幾個樂師來為我們演奏音樂。凱瑟琳趁大夥在欣賞表演時，上樓溜到希斯克里夫的房間。她喚著希斯克里夫，但沒有回應。她便爬上屋頂，從一個小窗戶鑽進房間裡。稍後，他們一起下樓來到廚房，我給希斯克里夫遞上晚餐，但他沒吃。

「納麗，君子報仇三年不晚，我一定要亨得利好看，只希望他不會太早死！」他說。

「希斯克里夫，人要學會寬恕！」我說。

「休想！我一定要報復個痛快！我要想一個好法子來報仇，一想到這裡，我就不會痛苦了。」

6. 凱瑟琳的選擇

P.52

納麗・狄恩繼續說道：

隔年夏天，離現在快二十三年囉，亨得利和法蘭絲的兒子出生了，名字叫做哈里登・恩蕭。那是一個可愛、健康的小寶寶，可是在他出生後不久，法蘭絲就去世了，於是由我來負責照顧寶寶。

妻子的去世，讓亨得利變了一個人。他意志消沉，開始酗酒賭博。他對待僕人很苛刻，沒多久僕人都離開了。他對希斯克里夫也很刻薄，但希斯克里夫忍了下來。看到亨得利愈來愈頹廢，希斯克里夫似乎很痛快。

山莊沒有訪客，除了艾德加・林頓，他偶而會來找凱瑟琳。凱瑟琳十五歲時，已經是鄉間的女王了！我不再喜歡她，她太傲慢跋扈了！

凱瑟琳過著雙面人的生活。在林頓一家人的面前，她會表現出淑女的樣子，禮貌周到，但在家裡和希斯克里夫在一起時，就會換回野孩子的樣子。

一天下午，凱瑟琳和希斯克里夫待在起居室裡時，艾德加來訪，希斯克里夫隨即離開。我留在起居室裡，因為亨德利不要凱瑟琳和艾德加獨處。

P.53

我把小哈里登放在地板上，然後開始收拾盤子。

「納麗，你待在這裡做什麼？」凱瑟琳口氣很差地說道。

「小姐，我在幹活。」我回答。

她從我身後走過來，在我耳邊沒好氣地說：「你出去！有訪客來訪時，僕人不應該在房間裡收拾東西。」

她以為艾德加看不到，便搶過我手上的抹布，然後在我的手臂上使勁地捏了一下。

「噢，好痛！小姐，你幹嘛這樣捏我？」我大聲叫道。

「我又沒有碰你！」她大喊道，耳朵氣得通紅。

「那這個是什麼？」我伸出手讓她看手臂上的紅印子。

凱瑟琳氣得甩了我一巴掌。

「凱瑟琳！親愛的凱瑟琳！」艾德加看到她的暴力行為，震驚地說道。

「納麗，你給我出去！」她大喊道。

哈里登嚇得放聲大哭。

凱瑟琳突然一把抓住哈里登，用力搖晃。艾德加想把孩子拉走，結果也被她打到。

我抱起哈里登，走進廚房。從起居室的門，我看艾德加拿起了他的帽子。

P. 55

「你要去哪裡？」凱瑟琳質問道：「你不可以走！」

「我非走不可！」他平靜地回答。

「不要，還不要走，坐下！如果你就這麼被我氣走了，我整晚都會很難過，我不想因為你而難過！」她說。

「我為你感到羞恥，我再也不會過來了！」他說完，便走到門口。

凱瑟琳撲倒在椅子上，唏哩嘩啦哭了起來。艾德加這時已經走出門外，卻突然一個轉身，奔回起居室，並把起居室的門帶上。

沒多久，外面傳來亨得利的馬匹聲音，我便去通報凱瑟琳和艾德加。當我看到他們時，我知道他們已經不再是單純的朋友，他們現在是一對情侶了。

突然，我聽到亨得利進屋的聲音，便連忙走回廚房裡，想把小哈里登藏起來，因為孩子很怕他。不過來不及了，

亨得利蹣跚地走進屋子，他喝醉了。

「你被我抓到了吧！」他抓起孩子叫道：「來，親我一個，不然我就扭斷你的脖子！」他大聲喊道。

可憐的哈里登嚇得尖叫。

我看著亨得利把孩子抱上樓，然後在上面的樓梯口停住，把孩子舉到欄杆外，懸在手上。

P. 56

「不要！」我大喊道，連忙跑上去救孩子。當我趕上去時，樓下傳來聲音。

是希斯克里夫。亨得利看了一下希斯克里夫，緊接著，哈里登掉了下去。

事情發生得太突然，我還來不及驚嚇，好在希斯克里夫設法接住了孩子。

我奔下樓，把孩子抱過來，哈里登連哭都沒哭。

亨得利慢慢走下樓，在玻璃杯倒了一些白蘭地，一飲而盡，然後喊道：「滾！你們都滾出去！」

希斯克里夫跟隨我走進廚房，然後打開後門。

「真希望他把自己喝死。」他邊說，邊走出門。

我坐了下來。

「納麗，你一個人在這裡嗎？」一個聲音悄悄地說道，那是凱瑟琳。

「是的，小姐。」我回答。

她走進廚房，跟我一起坐在壁爐旁。她面露憂色，我知道她有話要跟我說。我心裡頭對她還有氣，所以繼續顧著對哈里登哼搖籃曲。

「希斯克里夫呢？」她問。

「去馬房幹活了。」

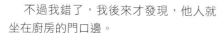

不過我錯了，我後來才發現，他人就坐在廚房的門口邊。

「天啊！我很不開心。」她喊道：「納麗，你可以幫我保密嗎？」

P. 57

「要看情況。」

「艾德加‧林頓今天跟我求婚，我答應了。」

「那你幹嘛不開心？你哥會高興，林頓家的人也不會反對，那還什麼問題？」

「這裡！還有這裡！」她大喊道，一隻手捶著前額，一隻手捶著胸口，「問題在我的靈魂、我的心裡，我正在走錯誤的一步！艾德加‧林頓不是我心裡面那個人，可是我又不能嫁給希斯克里夫，那樣只會降低我的身分地位。他沒有錢，看不到未來，這都是亨得利害的。」

真命天子？

- 想像一下你是凱瑟琳，為什麼艾德加‧林頓不是她婚姻上的真命天子？那希斯克里夫是嗎？把答案寫下來。
- 凱瑟琳嫁給艾德加和希斯克里夫之後生活，會各有何不同？

這時，門外有一點動靜，我轉頭一看，是希斯克里夫，他正舉步離開。凱瑟琳沒有發現，仍滔滔不絕地說著。

P. 59

「但是，納麗，如果我嫁給艾德加，那我就是有錢人了，可以幫希斯克里夫擺脫掉我哥。納麗，我就是希斯克里夫啊，他一直住在我心裡。」

這時，喬瑟夫走進門，我得開始做晚飯了。晚飯張羅好了之後，我去外頭叫希斯克里夫來吃飯，但是找不到他的人。從那之後，我們闊別了一段很長的時間之後才又重逢。

納麗‧狄恩到此講完了第一部分的前塵往事。

139

7. 再見希斯克里夫

P. 60

從荒野走回來的隔天早上，我發著高燒醒來。我病得很重，要在床上休養一個月。我現在感覺是好了些，不過還沒有力氣閱讀。我一個人百無聊賴，便請狄恩太太過來把房東的故事講完。

狄恩太太帶了針線活過來，一邊做女紅，一邊跟我說。

納麗・狄恩繼續說道：

希斯克里夫離開之後，凱瑟琳發燒病了好一段時間。林頓家的人想照顧她，便把她接到畫眉山莊。未料，林頓先生和林頓夫人也接連發燒，幾天內就雙雙去世了。

凱瑟琳在畫眉山莊待了幾個月，等她回來時又變了一個人。她的脾氣變得更差，有時對待我和其他的僕人甚是惡劣。

總之，三年之後，她嫁給了艾德加。他們要我跟著離開咆哮山莊，一起來畫眉山莊。我一開始不肯，因為我不想離開小哈里登，但是亨得利不要我留下來，所以我只好離開。

凱瑟琳嫁過來之後，脾氣收斂了些，大概是因為她可以為所欲為。

P. 61

我猜林頓先生怕她生氣，所以不想招惹她。她悶悶不樂時，林頓先生也就靜靜不作聲；她笑時，他就跟著她笑。兩人看起來滿幸福的。

幸福

- 你想凱瑟琳和艾德加過得幸福嗎？
- 說一下你感覺幸福的時光。這時你是和誰在一起的？你們在做什麼？

不過，花無百日紅。九月一個晚上，我從花園提著一籃蘋果回來時，我身後傳來一個聲音：「納麗，是你嗎？」

我轉過身，看到後面站著一個身材高大、膚色黝黑的男人。

「我在這裡等了一個小時了。」

他走近我，我看到他的眼睛，是希斯克里夫。

「真的是你？你回來了？」我叫道。

「我要跟凱瑟琳說說話，納麗，你去叫她來！跟她說村子裡來了一個人，有話要跟她講。」

凱瑟琳和艾德加這時正坐在客廳裡，氣氛很和諧，我很不想去破壞。不過，我還是跟凱瑟琳傳了話，凱瑟琳於是起身下樓。

P. 63

「是誰？」林頓先生問我。

「是住在恩蕭先生家的那個男孩——希斯克里夫。」我回答。

「什麼？那個吉普賽人？」他叫道。

幾分鐘後，凱瑟琳激動地跑上樓。

「哦，艾德加，艾德加！」她衝進門大聲說道：「希斯克里夫回來了！哦，我好高興！我可以讓他上來嗎？」

艾德加的臉色變得很凝重。

「凱瑟琳，請冷靜一點！沒有必要這麼興奮，他不過是個出走的僕人。」他說：「納麗，你去叫他上來吧。」

希斯克里夫這時待在廚房裡，在爐火的火光下，他的模樣更清楚了。他直直挺地站著，像個軍人一樣，而且神情慧黠，看起來意氣風發的。

我們走上樓來到客廳，他選了凱瑟琳對面的椅子坐了下來。凱瑟琳用充滿愛意的眼神看著他，而他也是，每一次看她時都非常的深情。顯然地，他們兩人對彼此的重逢都感到無比的興奮，艾德加看在眼裡，很不是滋味。

一個鐘頭之後，希斯克里夫告辭。臨走前，他跟我說他現在住在咆哮山莊。

一聽到這裡，我很震驚、很害怕。

當晚，凱瑟琳跑來我的房間，想跟我聊希斯克里夫。她跟我說了希斯克里夫為什麼會待在咆哮山莊的原因。

P. 64

「他想離畫眉山莊近一點，這樣我們就可以常常見面了。他會給我哥房租，我哥會接受的，他欠了一屁債，需要錢。」

從那天起，希斯克里夫就常常來畫眉山莊。林頓先生很不高興他來，可是他又希望凱瑟琳開心。的確，凱瑟琳現在對誰都很好、很貼心。

然而，沒多久，就看得出來伊莎貝拉喜歡上了希斯克里夫。伊莎貝拉芳年十八，出落得亭亭玉立。她敏銳聰明，但畢竟還是個孩子，直把希斯克里夫當成是一位斯文的白馬王子。

希斯克里夫並不喜歡伊莎貝拉，他眼裡只有凱瑟琳。艾德加很擔心，而且知道是希斯克里夫在勾引妹妹對他動心的。

看得出來伊莎貝拉開始變得鬱鬱寡歡，她食不下嚥，日漸消瘦憔悴。她對每一個人都很不滿，特別是對艾德加和凱瑟琳。她說，哥哥不管她，凱瑟琳對她也不好。凱瑟琳聽了很生氣。

「你幹嘛這樣說？我是什麼時候虧待你了？」凱瑟琳質問道。

「就像昨天，我們和希斯克里夫一起去荒野散步，結果你叫我走開，到別的地方去。」伊莎貝拉嗚咽地說道。

「那是因為我怕你無聊。」

P. 65

「才怪！你要我走開，是因為你知道我想和……」

「什麼？」凱瑟琳說。

「和他在一起！和希斯克里夫在一起！可是你只想自己一個人霸占他！你不要

141

他愛上別人。」

「伊莎貝拉，你是說，你希望希斯克里夫會愛上你？」

「我對希斯克里夫的愛，勝過你對艾德加的愛。如果你不要從中阻止，搞不好他就會愛上我！」

「你這個小笨蛋！你根本不知道他是什麼樣一個人。納麗，你跟她說說希斯克里夫這個人吧！就告訴她，他是個野蠻兇殘的人，就像野獸一樣。跟她說，他是一個毫不留情的人，讓她知道，他不可能愛上姓林頓的人。」

伊莎貝拉很生氣地瞪著凱瑟琳。

「我才不相信，是因為你有私心，才會這樣說。」

「好吧！那就隨便你！我無所謂！」凱瑟琳說完就走出房間，伊莎貝拉一時眼淚潰堤。

凱瑟琳和希斯克里夫

- 你想，凱瑟琳是想保護伊莎貝拉，還是想一個人霸占希斯克里夫？
- 她為什麼會說希斯克里夫不可能喜歡上姓林頓的人？
- 為什麼希斯克里夫會有可能娶伊莎貝拉？

P. 66

隔天，希斯克里夫來訪時，凱瑟琳和伊莎貝拉正在坐書房裡。他們還在生彼此的氣，氣氛顯得凝重。凱瑟琳一看到希斯克里夫，便跳起來跑過去迎接他。

「快進來，我們兩個人今天都很高興能看到你！」她笑笑地說：「希斯克里夫，有人比我還仰慕你，不是喔，我不是說納麗喔，我是說我的小姑！」

伊莎貝拉顯得很難為情，起身準備走開。

「別走，伊莎貝拉，不要走！」凱瑟琳緊緊地抓住女孩的手臂，「希斯克里夫，我們昨天才為你吵過架。伊莎貝拉說她喜歡你，而且她對你的愛，勝過艾德加對我的愛。」

伊莎貝拉的臉一陣白、一陣紅，眼底打轉著淚水。凱瑟琳放開她的手，她連忙跑出房間。

「你是說真的嗎？」希斯克里夫問。

「真的，她都為你害相思啦。」凱瑟琳說：「不過，別管她，我只是想給她一點顏色瞧瞧，看她還敢不敢忤逆我。我喜歡她，並不想傷害她。」

「我對她毫無興趣。」希斯克里夫說。

沉默半晌之後，希斯克里夫問道：「她是她哥哥的財產繼承人，對吧？」

「如果我們有小孩，那就不是。」凱瑟琳回答道，然後又補充了幾句：「希斯克里夫，你太關心你鄰居的財產了！你要記住，你這位鄰居的財產是我的！」

P. 67

在這之後，我決定要多多留意希斯克里夫，我不信任他這個人，也不信任凱瑟琳！

希斯克里夫再來訪時，伊莎貝拉正在外面的庭院裡。我站在廚房的窗戶旁邊，但他們看不到我。希斯克里夫走向伊莎貝拉，說了幾句話。伊莎貝拉很難為情地想要走開，但希斯克里夫攔住了她，然後向房子這邊瞄了一下，緊接著就抱住她，親了下去。

「背信的人！」我叫道。

「納麗，你在説誰？」是凱瑟琳，她就站在我的後面。

8. 希斯克里夫的復仇記

P. 68

納麗‧狄恩繼續説道：

凱瑟琳往窗外望去，目睹了希斯克里夫和伊莎貝拉在一起。

一會兒後，希斯克里夫打開廚房的門走進來，凱瑟琳正在那裡等著他。

「我叫你離她遠一點，否則我就跟艾德加告狀，那你以後就別想進門了。」凱瑟琳很生氣，但仍平靜地説。

「如果凱瑟琳想要我吻她，我何樂而不為？我又不是你丈夫，你吃什麼醋！」他回答。

「誰吃你的醋啊！你要是愛伊莎貝拉，就去娶她啊！」凱瑟琳激動地回答。

「但林頓先生會怎麼説呢？他不會讓希斯克里夫娶他妹妹的。」我説。

「誰管他答不答應！」希斯克里夫吼道，然後盯著凱瑟琳看。

「凱瑟琳，如果你以為我會相信你的甜言蜜語，那你就是笨蛋。你這樣對我，我很快就會向你報復。我還得感謝你跟我説你小姑的祕密，讓我心生妙計。」

他們繼續爭吵，我逕自走開，上樓去看林頓先生。

「納麗，你有看到夫人嗎？」我走進書房時，他問道。

P. 69

「有，先生，她在廚房裡，和希斯克里夫在一起。」我回答。

我跟他説了庭院睹見的那一幕，還有夫人和希斯克里夫的爭吵。

「先生，我想你應該出面。」我補充道。

他急急跑下樓，進到廚房裡。

「希斯克里夫，你出去！以後不要再來了，這裡不歡迎你！」他對訪客吼道。

艾德加的氣話讓凱瑟琳很難過，凱瑟琳要我帶她上樓。

「納麗，我頭好痛！你跟艾德加説我病了，不想見他。」她説。

不過我沒有奉命照做，一會兒後，他走進了她的房間，我站在房間外面聽著動靜。

「你以後還要再跟希斯克里夫見面嗎？」他冷靜地問。

「我不想談這件事。」她冷冷地回答。

「你是要我，還是希斯克里夫？你不能同時跟我們兩個人做朋友，你只能選一個。」他説。

這太為難凱瑟琳了。

「你不要在我旁邊！走開！」她尖叫

道。

　　接下來幾天，她把自己關在房裡，不肯吃東西。到了第三天，我給她送上一些吐司時，她餓得狼吞虎嚥，然後問道：「艾德加呢？」

P.70

　　「他在書房裡，他這幾天都在看書。」我回答。

　　聽到艾德加竟然沒有花時間來操心她，她難以忍受，整個脾氣發作起來。她氣得抓狂，用牙齒撕咬枕頭，然後要我把窗戶打開。

　　現在是隆冬之際，外面的風很大，我不肯遵命。她立刻哭了起來，開始把整個房間撒得到處都是枕頭的羽毛。我已經對她失去耐性了。

　　「不要再扔那些羽毛了！躺下，你要休息！」我嚴厲地說道。

　　我在房間裡四處撿拾羽毛，她這時安靜了些。

　　「我記得我在咆哮山莊的床。」她用含糊的聲音說：「我記得窗戶旁邊那些樅樹被風吹動的聲音，我想感受一下風。納麗，一下下就好！」

　　我不想再讓她難受，就把窗戶打開。冷風灌進來，在房間裡打轉。我很快再把窗戶關上，凱瑟琳躺在床上哀泣了起來。

　　「我待在房間裡多久了？」她哽咽道。

　　「小姐，三天了。」我回答。

　　「納麗，再把窗戶打開，不要關上！」

　　「不行，小姐，你會著涼的。」

　　「那我自己來開。」

P.72

　　我還沒能阻止她，她就跳下床，把窗戶打開，將頭探了出去。

　　我想把她拉開，可是她的力氣比我大。我四處看著有什麼東西可以披在她肩上，這時林頓先生走了進來。

　　「噢，先生，可憐的夫人病了，卻不肯待在床上，你得想想辦法啊。」我喊道。

　　「凱瑟琳病了？納麗，把窗戶關上！」他說：「凱瑟琳？」

　　她轉過頭看他，他認不出來眼前這個臉色憔悴蒼白的人，不禁楞了一會兒。緊接著，他牽起她的手，緊緊地摟住她。

　　「先生，她需要靜養，我們要小心不要再惹她生氣了。」

　　「納麗，我不需要你跟我講什麼。她會生病，也是你造成的，是你慫恿我去惹她生氣的，你為什麼要跟我說希斯克里夫和伊莎貝拉的事？」他說。

「我只是在做一個盡職的僕人該做的事。」我說。

凱瑟琳突然尖叫道：「對！納麗是我的敵人，她是奸細，是女巫！」

她掙開林頓先生的手，想過來打我，我趕緊跑出房間。

「她需要看醫生了。」我想。

我披上斗篷，往村子裡走去。

當我經過花園時，我看到了一個白白的東西在晃動，我走過去一瞧，竟然是伊莎貝拉的小狗！

P. 73

小狗被吊在花園的樹上，脖子上栓著繩子，幾乎快斷氣了。

我趕緊把小狗放下來，讓牠站起來。這時，遠遠地傳來馬蹄聲，半夜清晨兩點竟會有馬蹄聲，這是很不尋常的。我加緊腳步前去找醫生。

納麗所看到和所聽到的

• 你想，是誰想傷害伊莎貝拉的小狗？為什麼？
• 納麗聽到的馬蹄聲又是誰的馬？馬要往哪裡去？

我跟醫生描述凱瑟琳的狀況，醫生決定立刻出診。

「她已經三天沒有吃東西，而且行為舉止像發瘋了一樣。」我說。

「我聽說希斯克里夫回來了，這是真的嗎？」醫生問。

「是真的。他常常來畫眉山莊，不過我家主人不准他再來了。主人很擔心伊莎貝拉，因為她愛上了希斯克里夫。」

P. 74

「伊莎貝拉真是傻啊！林頓先生要把伊莎貝拉看好才是，村子裡有人說，今天晚上才看到她和希斯克里夫在一起，說看到他們在畫眉山莊後面的原野上散步，而且還聽到希斯克里夫要伊莎貝拉跟他私奔。」醫生說。

醫生說的消息嚇到了我，我想到了剛剛的馬蹄聲。我連忙跑回家，衝到伊莎貝拉的房間，房間裡沒有人！我一時不知如何是好，我應該去跟主人報告嗎？這個時機又不太對，他正在為凱瑟琳的事操煩，於是我決定先不說了。

醫生在返回村子之前，跟林頓先生和我交代了一下。

「林頓夫人沒有性命的危險，只要多多靜養，就會好起來。」他說。

隔天早上，住在村子裡的一位女僕跟林頓先生說了伊莎貝拉和希斯克里夫的事。

林頓先生起先不相信，但最後他說：「伊莎貝拉愛上哪兒，就上哪兒，以後不要在我面前提到她的名字。」

9. 凱瑟琳去世

P. 75

納麗・狄恩繼續說道：

凱瑟琳病了兩個月，這期間主人整天守候在側。凱瑟琳的身體終於開始有起色，主人這才放寬心。他一心希望她能夠完全康復——不只是因為他愛她，也是因為她懷孕了——那是他的繼承人！

伊莎貝拉出走六個星期後，給她哥哥捎來了一封短箋，説她結婚了，而且很抱歉傷害了他，請求他原諒。但主人沒有回她信。

幾天後，我收到了她寫給我的一封信，信就在我這裡，我可以讀給你聽，洛克伍德先生。

親愛的納麗：

我知道凱瑟琳病了，我想寫信問候她，但我沒辦法。我哥哥沒有回我信，所以我寫給你。請跟我哥哥說，我愛他，也想念他。

我昨晚抵達了咆哮山莊。納麗，我想問你兩個問題：

一、你怎麼有辦法待在這裡而沒有瘋掉？這裡一點點人味都沒有。

二、希斯克里夫到底是人還是魔？納麗，我嫁的到底是什麼？

我恨他！請不要跟畫眉山莊的任何人提這件事。你快來這裡找我吧！

伊莎貝拉

P. 76

我跟林頓先生説我收到來信，他准許我過去。

我來到山莊時，伊莎貝拉和希斯克里夫兩個人都在起居室。伊莎貝拉臉色蒼白，頭髮凌亂，希斯克里夫看起來安好無恙。我環顧了一下四周，房間髒亂不堪，四處都是灰塵。

伊莎貝拉沒有收到艾德加的回信，很是失望。希斯克里夫立刻跟我問起凱瑟琳的事。

「林頓夫人的身體正在復原，但她的模樣和性格都變了，林頓先生現在只能懷念當初愛上的那位女子。不過他當然會對她不離不棄，她好歹是他的妻子，這是他的責任。」我説。

明顯可以看出來希斯克里夫在極力按捺住自己翻攪的情緒。

P. 77

「納麗，你在回去之前，一定要答應我，幫我們安排見一次面。我要見她，一定要見到她！懂嗎？」

「你不可以見她，我不會幫這個忙的！她就要把你忘掉了，再看到你，只會讓她再受到刺激。」我回答。

「忘掉我！納麗，你明明知道這是不可能的。她想我，比想艾德加多得多了。」

「凱瑟琳和艾德加很恩愛，你不要這樣説我哥哥！」伊莎貝拉叫道。

「你哥愛你有像愛她那樣嗎？」希斯克里夫口氣不屑地説：「你離家出走時，他有感到要緊嗎？他這個時候又有來關心你嗎？」

「他不知道我現在過得是什麼樣的生活。」

「納麗，我們要從畫眉山莊私奔離開時，我把她的小狗吊起來，而她竟然對我的暴力行為沒有感覺。現在，我終於讓她恨我了。」

他拉住伊莎貝拉的手臂，把她從房間推出去。

「你上樓！我要跟納麗講一些話。」他大喊道。

他想安排和凱瑟琳見面的事宜，洛克伍德先生，我拒絕了五十次，但最後，我還是讓步了。

「艾德加下次要出門時，你通知我，我就過去。」他一說，一邊遞給我一封要給凱瑟琳的信，「納麗，一定要確保沒有其他人在，答應我！」

P. 79

我一直等到星期天大家都去上教堂時，才把信轉交給林頓夫人。

那天天氣很暖和，所有的窗戶和門都敞開著，好讓新鮮的空氣進來。夫人這時就坐在客廳裡，她穿著一件白色的洋裝，肩膀上披著一條披肩。她臉色蒼白，眼神空洞，神情恍惚。

「林頓夫人，這裡有一封信要給你。」

我輕聲地說：「你現在就把信讀了，還等著回信呢。是希斯克里夫寫給你的信。」

她露出苦惱的神色，困惑了一會兒，然後才把信拿起來讀。她嘆了口氣，用手指著信的署名，盯著我瞧。

「他現在就在花園裡，我要叫他進來嗎？」我說。

不過倒不勞煩我了，大門敞開著，希斯克里夫隨即大步走了進來，他將凱瑟琳摟進懷裡，親吻了她好長的時間。他沒有直瞅她的臉──他做不到。跟我一樣，他知道她活不久了。

「噢，凱瑟琳！噢，我的性命！」他喊道。

凱瑟琳這時把他推開，說道：「希斯克里夫，你和艾德加都傷透了我的心！現在，你們卻都想要我憐憫你們，我不會的！你殺了我，但你還這麼健康，我死了以後，你還打算活多久？」

P. 80

希斯克里夫的眼神充滿著痛苦。

「你會忘掉我嗎？我埋在土裡時，你快樂得起來嗎？」她繼續說道：「二十年後，你會不會說：『這是凱瑟琳‧恩蕭的墓，我很久以前愛過她。』希斯克里夫，你會這樣說嗎？」

「凱瑟琳，不要這樣折磨我，我不可能忘掉你的。」他叫道。

「那我們為什麼不能永遠在一起？」她低吟道。

他站起身挪步，不想讓她看到自己的臉。

「希斯克里夫！」她叫道。

她很虛弱，但還是硬站了起來。

他轉過身來，眼裡泛著淚光。她想衝過去，但跌倒了。他躍步過來扶住她，緊緊將她摟在懷裡。

「凱瑟琳，你為什麼要離開我？不是我讓你心碎的，是你讓自己心碎的。你讓自己心碎，也隨之讓我心碎。沒有你，我要怎麼活下去？」他叫道。

你讓我心碎

- 在這個用法中，heart 使用的動詞是 break。從下的選項中選出正確的動詞搭配。
  - a) 把你的腳「留」/「放」在裡面（用來表達說難為情的事，或做難為情的事）
  - b)「拉」/「推」某人的腳（用來表達對某人開玩笑）
  - c)「給」/「拿」某人一個伸手（幫助某人）

P. 81

「不要說了！不要說了！如果是我的錯，我就以死謝罪！夠了！你也遺棄過我，但我原諒了你！」凱瑟琳哽泣道。

這時，我看到窗外的路上站了一群人，是林頓先生和僕人們，他們剛從教堂回來。

「主人回來了，你得走了，希斯克里夫，快走！」我喊道。

凱瑟琳緊緊抱住希斯克里夫，不讓他走。

「我等會兒會再來，」希斯克里夫跟她說：「我會一直待在花園裡。」

「不要！不要走！」她在他耳邊說道，緊緊抱住不放。

「只走開一個鐘頭。」

「一分鐘也不行！」

「我一定得走，艾德加很快就會進來了。」

「不要！噢，不要！不要走！希斯克里夫，我就要死了！我要死了！」

「噓！噓！凱瑟琳，那我就留下來，就算他一槍把我斃了，能在你身邊死去，我也會很幸福。」

這時凱瑟琳朝著他倒了下去，他趕緊用手臂扶住她。

「她不是昏厥過去，就是死了。」我想。

艾德加走進來時，臉色頓時刷白。希斯克里夫走向他，手裡抱著凱瑟琳攤死的身子。

「好好照顧她，有話之後再說。」他說。

那天半夜十二點左右，凱瑟琳的孩子呱呱墜地了。我們用她母親的名字來為她命名。在她出生兩個鐘頭後，她的母親撒手人寰了。

10. 咆哮山莊的新主人

P. 82

納麗・狄恩繼續說著故事：

第二天破曉之際，我去找希斯克里夫，一定得告訴他這個噩耗，我想盡快把這件事情了結掉。當我找到他的時候，他就站在花園的一棵樹下。

他仰著頭，說：「我知道。」

他陷入極大的痛苦中，我看了很難過。

「是怎麼……？」

他打住，喊不出她的名字。他在和悲

働交戰，最後好不容易終於開口問：「她走得如何？」

「很平靜，像隻小羊。她現在安息了。」

「不，凱瑟琳·恩蕭，我還活著，你不能安息！你說是我殺了你，那你的鬼魂就來找我啊！死者會對殺害他們的人陰魂不散，你要一直跟著我！沒有靈魂，我活不下去！」他叫喊道。

他把頭往後仰，像隻野獸一樣地咆哮著。

凱瑟琳的鬼魂

• 凱瑟琳安息了嗎？還是她如希斯克里夫所希望的，陰魂不散？回到故事的最前面去檢查看看。

P.83

隨後的那個星期五變天了，刮起了寒風，開始降雪。

林頓先生在樓上睡覺，我和寶寶在客廳裡。這時，伊莎貝拉突然衝了進來，她頭髮濕答答的，衣服都是泥濘。

她沒有穿外套，沒有戴帽子，只穿著一件薄洋裝和一雙薄薄的鞋子。而在她的脖子上，有一道傷口。

「我是從咆哮山莊逃出來的！」她緩過氣來說：「叫僕人立刻準備馬車，納麗，我一定要離開這個地方。」

她一直到一切準備就緒，才感到滿意，願意把濕衣脫下，換上乾爽的衣服。接著，我給她端來一杯熱茶。

P.84

「納麗，我想跟你待在一起，可是希斯克里夫不會允許的，他怕我在畫眉山莊會過得很快樂，他希望我和他一起受苦。我想不透凱瑟琳為什麼會喜歡他，他是一個怪物！我是不會讓他殺了我的。」她說。

她開始哭了起來，然後又繼續說道：「希斯克里夫現在白天都把自己關在房間裡，到了晚上時就去荒野，清晨才回來。昨天，他從荒野回來時，亨得利和我正在客廳。當時前門是鎖上的，他進不來，就開始敲門，吵得亨得利很火大。

『讓他多待個五分鐘。』亨得利說完便站起來，從口袋裡掏出一把刀子。

『坐著，什麼話都不要說！』他對我說：『我要去宰了他，他搶了我、你和哈里登。他借我一大筆錢去賭錢，結果我輸了，咆哮山莊現在是他的了。』

這時，窗口突然出現希斯克里夫的臉，他的頭髮和衣服都覆著白雪，表情很可怕。他用手臂猛力敲打窗戶，把玻璃都敲破了。

『你不要進來！亨得利拿著刀，想要殺你！』我叫道。

這時亨得利已經望著窗戶這邊衝過來，刀口對著希斯克里夫的脖子刺過去，但希斯克里夫抓抓住了他的手。刀子一轉，就深深刺進了亨得利的手腕，傷口立刻湧出鮮血，亨得利隨即倒地。

P. 86

希斯克里夫從窗戶跳進來，抓住亨得利的肩膀，將他的頭往石板地撞了幾下，然後又突然住手。他在亨得利的傷口紮了一條布，然後不發一語地走出房間。

今天早上，我下樓時，看到亨得利和希斯克里夫已經在廚房裡了。他們兩個人的氣色都很差，看到希斯克里夫這麼虛弱的樣子，我感到自己變強壯了。我要讓他好看，一定要讓他好看。」

「小姐，這樣不太好。」我說。

「納麗，是他先傷害我的。而且他從不道歉，我沒有機會原諒他。」

伊莎貝拉喝了口茶後，繼續說道。

「我給亨得利遞上水，『你沒事吧？』我問他說：『他害死了你妹妹，現在也想把你幹掉。』

希斯克里夫聽到了我說的話，他嘆口氣說：『滾！不要讓我看到你！』

希斯克里夫的臉上流著淚水，突然之間我不再怕他了。

『我也愛凱瑟琳，在你返鄉之前，她一直都很快樂。』我說。

我的話激怒了他，他想對我動粗，但我離他很遠，他便拿了一把刀子扔向我，刺中了我耳朵下面這個地方。我把刀子拔出來，對著他扔回去。

他從廚房那一邊對著我衝過來，但被亨得利給擋住，兩個人在一起摔到了地上。我趁著他們在打架之際，逃了出來，一路跑來這裡。不過，我現在得走了。」

P. 87

伊莎貝拉喝完茶後，就去了倫敦，沒有跟她哥哥告別。

她一去不回，但時常會給艾德加寫信。

在她逃離沒幾個月之後，她生了一個兒子。她將孩子取名做林頓。她說，孩子不是很健康，常常哭鬧。

林頓

• 你想伊莎貝拉為什麼要將兒子取名「林頓」？

• 林頓發生了什麼事？如果你不記得了，再回到故事的前面查看一下。

村子有人把伊莎貝拉在倫敦的住址給了希斯克里夫，可是希斯克里夫並沒有去看她們母子。

有一次，他跟我說：「等我需要孩子

時，我就會把孩子要回來。」

在凱瑟琳過世六個月之後，亨得利·恩蕭也去世了。那個晚上，他把自己鎖在房裡，喝得酩酊大醉。早上時，喬瑟夫把鎖敲掉，看到亨得利躺在地板上已經斷氣了，得年二十七歲，和我同年。

P. 88

他、凱瑟琳和我的童年往事，歷歷在目，我坐下來哭泣，彷彿他就是我的兄長一般。

我去咆哮山莊幫他料理後事，希斯克里夫沒有阻攔我。

在我們即將前往教堂的時候，希斯克里夫抱起哈里登，把他放在桌子上。

「你現在是我的了！」他靜靜地說。

小男孩對他笑了笑，我看了憂心忡忡，我不相信希斯克里夫這個人。

「他要跟我一起回畫眉山莊，他是林頓先生的外甥。」我說。

「他想要嗎？」

「他當然想要。」

「那你就跟他說，他如果要這個男孩，那另外那個孩子就會來補這個缺。」

當主人聽的時候就明白了，所以他再也不提哈里登的未來了。

希斯克里夫如今是咆哮山莊的主人，亨得利死後留下了一屁股債，所以哈里登什麼也沒得到，他成了在父親房子裡幹活的一個僕人。

另外那個孩子

· 希斯克里夫說的「另外那個孩子」，是指誰？

11. 表親

P. 89

納麗·狄恩繼續說道：

接下來的十二年，是我這一生中最快樂的時光。我照顧小凱希，我們叫她凱希，不叫她凱瑟琳。我們看著她長大。

她是一個漂亮的女孩，為這個令人哀傷的房子帶來了陽光。她遺傳了媽媽的黑眼珠，和林頓家的白皮膚、金頭髮。她天性溫和，不像她媽媽那樣個性強烈，容易激動。她聰明伶俐，學什麼都很快。她對希斯克里夫或咆哮山莊的事一無所知，因為她還不准走出山莊一步。

後來有一天，伊莎貝拉捎來了一封信，說她即將離世，想跟她哥哥見最後一面，並且希望哥哥能幫她照顧兒子。林頓先生於是立刻準備啟程前往倫敦。

「納麗，一定要把凱希看好，不要讓她跑出山莊，連你帶她出這個大門都不可以。」他對我叮囑道。

現在是夏天，凱希每天都會去外面玩耍。她會在山莊裡四處走動，或騎著她的小馬到處遊蕩，不過她茶點時間一定會回來。

我不擔心她，因為我知道大門上了鎖，她出不去。然而，這一天，她茶點時間竟然沒有回來，我趕緊出去找她。

「你有看到小姐嗎？」我問一個田地裡工人，他正在修理樹籬的破洞。

「有，她今天早上騎著小馬跳過樹籬，跑得不見人影了。」他回答。

洛克伍德先生，你可以想見我是什麼樣的心情！我從樹籬的破洞擠身出去，在路上來回走了幾趟，但都沒有找到她。

後來，我在路過咆哮山莊時，撞見了她的狗。我跑到房子門前，大聲地敲門。一個僕人開了門。

「你是來找你家小姐的嗎？別擔心，她在裡面，請進。」她說。

我走進門，看到凱希就坐在起居室裡，正在和哈里登有說有笑的。哈里登現在是一個十八歲大的小夥子了，高頭大馬的。他用訝異的表情看著凱希。

「小姐，你太淘氣了！以後不准你一個人在莊園裡玩了。」

「噢，納麗，我有好多事情要跟你說。」她開心地叫說：「你以前有進來過這個房子嗎？」

「戴上帽子，馬上回家！」我說。

「這是你家主人的房子嗎？」她問哈里登道。

哈里登低下眼，咒罵了一句，轉身離去。

「小姐，別再問了，我們走。」我輕聲地說。

在我們準備要走時，她轉頭跟哈里頓說：「把我的小馬牽過來，快點！」

「我又不是你的僕人，不要使喚我！」男孩吼道。

凱希這下子楞住了，在畫眉山莊，大家可把她侍候得像公主一樣。

「你這個討厭鬼！我要跟我爸講！」她說。

「小姐，你可不要害他。」管家對她說：「他雖然不是主人的兒子，但他可是你表哥啊。」

「表哥！」凱希叫道：「可是我爸才去倫敦接我表弟，我表弟是紳士的兒子，而這個……」

她打住，大哭了起來。

「噓！凱希小姐，你的表兄弟不只一位。走吧，我們回家。」我說。

在回畫眉山莊的路上，我要她答應，決不跟她爸爸說她去過咆哮山莊的事。

幾天後，我們收到林頓先生的信，伊莎貝拉已經去世了，他正帶著她的兒子正在返家的路上。要見到倫敦來的表弟，凱希很興奮。

「他才比我小六個月而已，能有人陪我玩，一定很棒！」她說。

林頓是一個蒼白柔弱的男孩，而且神情憂鬱。從倫敦長途來到這裡，他很疲倦，想要休息。

他躺在書房的沙發上，凱希一邊撫摸他的捲髮，一邊親吻他。林頓很歡喜，有氣無力地對她笑了笑。

P. 93

當晚稍後，希斯克里夫的僕人喬瑟夫來敲門，帶了消息要給林頓先生。

「希斯克里夫想把孩子要回去，我得把孩子帶走。」老人說。

艾德加‧林頓沉默了半晌，然後用平靜的口氣說：「跟希斯克里夫先生說，他兒子明天就會返回咆哮山莊。他現在已經上床了，他很累，走不了那麼遠的路。」

喬瑟夫沒有帶走孩子，便不肯離開，但林頓先生毅然地把他推出門外。

「那就讓希斯克里夫明天親自過來，再看你敢不敢把他推出門。」老人家大喊道。

我的主人看起來一臉愁容。

「納麗，明天一早，你就讓孩子坐凱希的小馬，回咆哮山莊。不要跟凱希說孩子去了哪裡，只要說他爸爸要見他就可以。」

我照辦了。接下來幾年，這對表姐弟就各自長大了。

凱希十六歲生日這一天，天氣風和日麗，她央求爸爸准許她去荒野散步。

我們於是出發走在往咆哮山莊那個方向的路上。凱希跑在我前面，尋找草叢中的鳥巢。

P. 95

後來，她不見人影一會兒，當我再看到她時，她正在和兩個人交談，一個是希斯克里夫，另一個是哈里登。咆哮山莊上的這片土地是屬於希斯克里夫的，我們算是入侵。我趕緊跑向他們。

「我只是想找鳥蛋。」她說：「你們是誰？我見過那個人，他是你兒子嗎？」她繼續說。

「不是，不過我有一個兒子，你見過。我住在那邊，過來坐坐再回家吧。」

「不行，不可以。」我在凱希的耳邊說。

「納麗，不要多話。哈里登，帶這位年輕的小姐回家！」希斯克里夫說。

我還不及發言，這兩個年輕人便開始朝屋子跑去。希斯克里夫和我跟在後面，我們一邊走，希斯克里夫一邊說他對林頓和凱希的打算，他想讓湊合他們兩個，讓他們成親。

「我會讓這件事成功。」他說。

我們抵達時，林頓正在起居室裡。他現在已經長得比凱希高，而且看起來也

比較健康。能再見到林頓，凱希感到很開心。

「我現在知道你住在這裡了，我以後每天都要來找你！」她跟林頓說。

「你父親不會樂見的，他不喜歡我，我們吵過架。」希斯克里夫說。

P. 96

「那麼林頓就來畫眉山莊找我。」她回答。

「我走不了四哩遠的路，那對我來說太遠了。」男孩說。

希斯克里夫用嫌棄的目光看了他一下。

「納麗，他很虛弱，凱希很快就會發現的。哈里登就不一樣了，他可壯了，但凱希不曾多看他一眼。他跟我以前一樣是個僕人，沒上過課，不識字，不會寫字，但他不是笨蛋。他在吃我吃過的苦頭。」

凱希這趟來咆哮山莊很開心，隔天，便不禁跟父親聊了起來。

「你為什麼不要我去找林頓？是因為你和希斯克里夫先生吵過架嗎？」她問。

「凱希，希斯克里夫是壞人，他恨一個人時，就會去毀掉那個人的生活。我不准你再去他那裡了。」父親回答。

凱希很愛父親，便順從了父親的話。不過，她開始偷偷寫信給林頓，他們魚雁往返，互相交換禮物，幾個月後被我在書房的抽屜發現了，他們最近寫的信是情書。

「林頓不會寫這種東西，這一定是希斯克里夫寫的。」我心想。

我把信丟進火堆，凱希發現後哭了，傷心了好一陣子。

12. 尾聲

P. 98

納麗・狄恩繼續說：

那年冬天，林頓先生得了重感冒，在床上休養了好幾個月。之後，我也發了三個星期的高燒。我們兩個人都由凱希來照顧——她真是一個天使！她每天不是陪她父親，就是陪我。晚上時，我們不需要她照料，而我也沒去想她晚上的時間是怎麼打發的。

有一晚，我感覺好些了，就來到她的房間，要跟她道晚安。結果，她不在房間裡。我在屋子裡找遍，都沒看她的人。

「她可能是去花園裡散步吧。」我心想。於是我回到她的房間裡等她。這晚月光皎潔，地上積了一些雪，接著，我看到了凱希，她正爬下她的小馬。一會兒後，她打開門走進來。

「凱希小姐，你上哪兒了？」我說。

154

「噢，納麗，你嚇到我了！」她喊道：「你不要生我的氣，我跟你說實話，我剛剛去了咆哮山莊。你和爸爸病倒了以後，我每天都過去。林頓的身體不是很好，他很喜歡我去陪他。你不要阻止我去看他，也請不要跟爸爸說這件事。」

「我想一下。」我回答：「你先睡吧。」

P.100

第二天早上，我把事情都跟主人說了。他說，一定不能再讓凱希偷偷跑去咆哮山莊了。

那是去年冬天的事，到了春夏相交之際，艾德加准許了凱希和林頓彼此通信。林頓央求凱希去看他，但艾德加不肯再讓她去咆哮山莊。最後，他同意讓兩人在咆哮山莊附近的一處荒原上相見。

「納麗，我病得很重，沒辦法跟著凱希一起去。你一定要跟著去，而且不能走離開荒原！」他說。

我們抵達時，林頓正躺在草地上。他看起來比之前更消瘦、更蒼白。

「林頓，你看起來不是很好，你的父親為什麼不幫你找醫生？」凱希對他說道。

男孩沒有回答。他閉上眼睛，把頭埋進胸前。

「他想睡覺！」凱希不耐煩地喊道：「納麗，他對我沒有興趣了！那他幹嘛還要跟我見面？」

男孩突然抬起頭來，喊道：「是我爸，他走過來了！」他很害怕，臉頰上滾下了淚水。「凱希，你不要走！你要是走了，他會殺了我！」

我聽到後面傳來聲音，我轉過頭去，是希斯克里夫。

「林頓，起來！不要哭了！」他吼道。

P.101

林頓很害怕，他想站起來，可是沒有氣力，結果往後摔倒在地上。

「凱希，你幫他扶起來吧，帶他回屋子裡。」希斯克里夫說。

我制止凱希，但她不聽我的話。

我們到了山莊時，凱希和林頓進了屋子，我留在屋外。我在一旁等著時，希斯克里夫突然把我推進屋內，然後把門鎖上。凱希和我被軟禁了！

「他為什麼要把我們鎖起來？他到底想對我們怎樣？」凱希問。

「父親要我們明天就結婚，他怕我很快就會死了，你們今晚只能待在這裡了。」林頓說。

「噢，可憐的爸爸，他一定會很擔心的！」凱希叫道。

這時，希斯克里夫轉了回來。他把林頓趕到樓上睡覺後，又把門鎖上，然後走到爐火旁站著，凱希就跟在他旁邊。

「我才不怕你！」凱希喊道：「把鑰匙

給我，我們要出去！」

凱希往前舉步，想從希斯克里夫的手把鑰匙拿過來。

P.103

「不要碰我！離我遠一點，不然我就揍你！」他大喊道：「我恨你！」

他的話讓我震驚，但我知道我不能透露任何事。

到了九點左右，他帶我們到樓上的一間臥室裡，然後把門鎖上。

隔天一早，希斯克里夫來把凱希帶走。

我在咆哮山莊裡被關了五夜四天，這期間我看到的人只有哈里登。他每天會給我帶一次食物過來，但從不開口說話。

到了第五天，管家季拉幫我開了門，放我出去。她在房間裡看到我，很是驚訝。

「所有人都以為你在荒野那邊走失了。」她說。

我快步下樓，在起居室裡看到了林頓。

「凱希呢？她走了嗎？」我問。

「她在樓上，被關在她的房間裡，不能離開，父親說她一定要跟我們住在這裡。她現在是我的妻子了。」他回答。

「你有她房間的鑰匙嗎？」

「有，放在樓上，不過我現在沒有力氣走上去拿。」

「希斯克里夫在哪裡呢？」

「他跟醫生在外面，他說我舅舅快死了。」

「林頓先生要死了！我一定要立刻回畫眉山莊。」我叫道。

P.104

我一路飛奔回去。僕人們看到我，又聽到凱希安全無恙，大家都很高興。我去看林頓先生，他躺在床上，臉色蒼白，面容憂愁。他看著我，用細微的聲音喊著凱希的名字。

「她就快回來了。」我說。

我正準備回咆哮山莊把凱希救出來時，凱希自己衝進了門，往父親的床邊奔去。她陪著父親，幾個鐘頭後，父親斷氣了。

希斯克里夫准許凱希待在畫眉山莊，等父親的葬禮結束之後再回來。葬禮那天稍晚，我們靜靜地坐在書房時，凱希跟我說她是怎麼逃出咆哮山莊的。

「林頓對我感到很抱歉，便開門讓我走。我趁天亮之前，從起居室的窗戶爬出來，一路跑回來。」她說。

這時，門突然被打開，希斯克里夫走了進來。凱希站起來想離開，但是希斯克里夫抓住她的手臂。

「不要再逃跑了！跟我回去！」他說。

「希斯克里夫先生，我會跟你回去，因為林頓是我在這世上唯一愛的人，而且我知道他也愛我。而你呢，你不愛別人，也沒有人愛你。我真慶幸我不是你！」她膽氣十足地說。

P.105

接著，她轉向我，小聲地說：「納麗，再會了！要來看我，別忘了！」

「納麗，我不准你進我的房子。」希斯克里夫一邊說，一邊把凱希拉出房間：「我有事要找你時，我會過來。」

從那天之後，我就沒再看過他們了。不過，季拉跟我說了後續的情況。

林頓的健康每況愈下，最後去世了。

葬禮過後，凱希把自己關在房間裡。希斯克里夫去找過她一次，讓她看林頓的遺囑。遺囑上寫著，這個男孩死後的財產全部歸父親所有，所以凱希的財產也連帶歸林頓的父親所有。現在，畫眉山莊已經屬於希斯克里夫的了。凱希呢，一無所有。

去世
• 將在這個悲劇故事中去世的人，列出清單，並說明原因。

納麗‧狄恩講完了故事。

P. 106

幾個星期過後，我恢復了力氣。時值一月中，我不想再待在這個寒冷荒涼的地方，便搬回倫敦。

九月時，我回到約克夏，決定去畫眉山莊拜訪納麗‧狄恩。我敲了門，一位老婦人出來應門。

「狄恩女士不住在這裡了，她現在在咆哮山莊。」她跟我說道。

現在時候還早，我便步行走過荒野，往山莊前進。

當我抵達時，我聽到敞開的窗戶傳出來說話聲，就走過去探個究竟。

是凱希和哈里登，他們正坐在桌前，前面放著一本書，哈里登在大聲唸著書。哈里登一身新衣服，樣子很英俊。

當他正確唸完一頁之後，凱希給了他一個吻。顯然地，這對表兄妹現在成了好朋友了。

我靜靜地走到屋後，在廚房裡看到了狄恩太太。她一看到我，好不驚訝。

「狄恩太太，你怎麼來咆哮山莊了？希斯克里夫的人呢？」我說。

「那麼說你是沒聽到風聲了，」她說：「他死了。」

「這是什麼時候的事？」

「三個月前的事。你坐下來，我說給你聽。」

P. 108

我坐定之後，她開始說道：季拉後來離開了咆哮山莊，希斯克里夫要我過來當管家。這讓凱希很開心，她開始和我、和哈里登長時間待在起居室裡。起初，她會嘲笑表哥不識字，但兩個人慢慢慢變成了好朋友，她就開始教他認字，而哈里登就幫她種花園。

一天晚上，只剩我和希斯克里夫獨處時，他問我說：「納麗，你有沒有注意到，他們兩個人都有像凱瑟琳一樣的眼睛？他們兩個人都會讓我起到凱瑟琳，我身邊的每一個東西都在提醒我，凱瑟琳曾經存在過，而我失去了她。」

從那時候開始，希斯克里夫的行為舉止就變得很奇怪。他晚上都會出門，一直到天亮了才會回來。他不吃不喝，有時只是坐在那裡，注視著前方，一臉滿足的樣子。

一天早上，我在屋子裡四處走動時，發現他房間的窗戶開敞著。外頭的雨下很大，我走過去把窗戶關上，而當時，躺在床上的希斯克里夫已經斷氣了。他的臉上有一抹微笑，一隻手擱在敞開的窗戶旁的架子上。

洛克伍德先生，村子裡的人說，他們在荒野上看過一個男鬼和一個女鬼在遊盪，不過我認為凱瑟琳和希斯克里夫現在已經安息了。

ANSWER KEY

Before Reading

Pages 8-9
1 1. b   2. d   3. a   4. c
3 a. Two.   b. 27.
c. Mr and Mrs Linton, Edgar Linton and Linton
   Heathcliff.
d. Heathcliff.
e. Hareton Earnshaw is Edgard Linton's nephew.
4 a. 4   b. 1   c. 5   d. 3   e. 2
5 a. Heathcliff.   b. Catherine Earnshaw.

Pages 10-11
6 a. 3   b. 2
8 a. 2   b. 1   c. 5   d. 3   e. 4
9 a. 4   b. 1   c. 3   d. 5   e. 2

Page 15
Because he was tall and handsome,
dressing like a gentleman but was dark
and also looked like a gypsy.

Page 23
Hareton Earnshaw is Catherine Earnshaw's
nephew.

Page 27 He loves and misses her.

Page 57
1. Edgar: She will lead a rich and comfortable
   but maybe boring life.
2. Heathcliff: She will lead a poor life and a life
   of work but of love and friendship.

Page 73
1. Heathcliff hurt the dog. He wanted revenge
   on the Lintons.
2. Isabella and Heathcliff were on the horses.
   They were going to get married in secret.

Page 80 a. put   b. pull   c. give

Page 82 Catherine's ghost haunts Heathcliff.

Page 87 1. To get back at Heathcliff, because he
hates the Linton family.
2. He marries Cathy Linton and then dies.

Page 88 Linton Heathcliff, Isabella's and

Heathcliff's son.

Page 105
• Mr and Mrs Earnshaw: illness
• Mr and Mrs Linton: illness
• Frances: illness
• Hindley: drinking and illness
• Edgar: illness
• Isabella: illness
• Catherine: broken heart
• Linton: illness

After Reading

Page 111
3
a. He adopts Heathcliff and cares for him as a
   son.
b. He is Heathcliff's tenant.
c. He is Heathcliff's neighbor and rival in love.
d. He is Heathcliff's son.
4
a. she is Catherine's housekeeper and confidante
b. she is Catherine's neighbor and later becomes
   her sister-in-law
c. she is her daughter
d. he is her nephew

Pages 112-113
5 a. T b. F c. F d. T e. T f. F g. F h. F
6
b. Mr Heathcliff greets him coldly but offers him
   wine. Heathcliff's dogs attack him.
c. She was her servant and housekeeper.
f. He told Heathcliff not to come back to
   Thrushcross Grange.
g. Heathcliff owned Wuthering Heights because
   Hindley sold it to him because of his debts.
h. He wanted his son Linton to marry Catherine
   Linton so he would inherit Thrushcross
   Grange.
7
a. Hindley hit Heathcliff with this when they were
   young boys.
b. Heathcliff threw this at Edgar when he came
   to Wuthering Heights and insulted him.
c. Catherine rips her pillow and throws the
   feathers around the room when she is upset

8 a. brother, uncle   b. nephew, son
c. cousin   d. aunt, sister-in-law
9 a. Wild but quiet.   b. Angry and vindictive.
10
a. Catherine Earnshaw is dark-haired, wild,
   quick-tempered and passionate but marries
   Edgar who is safe and rich.
   Isabella Linton is blond, sensible and calm
   but then falls in love with Heathcliff, not
   realizing what he is like and marries him, but
   she then regrets doing so.
b. Hareton is wild but strong and has suffered
   in the care of Heathcliff but then finds love
   with Cathy Linton.
   Linton Heathcliff is sickly child who is always
   pale and sad. He is weak and scared of
   Heathcliff.
11 It can be confusing but makes the family
ties, passions and problems more dramatic and
tragic.
12
• Catherine Earnshaw is passionate about
  Heathcliff but selfish and wants everyone and
  everything to be as she wants.
• Edgar Linton is caring and good but weak
  and unable to stand up to Catherine or
  Heathcliff.
• Hindley Earnshaw loves and then misses his
  wife when she dies and he is unable to accept
  Heathcliff as a brother.
• Isabella Linton is stupid to falls for Heathcliff
  but then strong when she runs away and
  looks after her son on her own.
• Nelly Dean is caring but distant and judging.
13
a. They care for each other but are not great
   friends.
b. They are close as brother and sister and look
   after each other as much as they can.
c. They like and respect each other. They try to
   not be involved in the previous generation's
   problems.
14 b
15 a. working class
b. gentry (upper-middle class)

c. working class
d. gentry (upper-middle class)

16 a. 5   b. 9   c. 8   d. 10   e. 11   f. 6
g. 2   h. 3   i. 12   j. 7   k. 1   l. 4
17
a. passionate and eternal
b. brotherly and protective
c. forced by Heathcliff, not natural
d. devotion
19
He helped in Hindley's downfall, took their
inheritance and then treated their heir, Hareton,
as Hindley had treated him. He married Isabella
and took her away from the family and then
forced his son to marry the Linton heir so he
could own their property as well.
20 A few examples
(Page 13) The house stands on the top of a hill.
On one side of it there are a few trees. They all
lean in the same direction, blown by the strong
north winds.
(Page 16) It was snowing heavily now and I was
very cold. I tried to open the door but it was
locked.
(Page 27) I'm glad he did because the snow
was like a white ocean and it was impossible to
see the road.
On the moor they were free from social and
family conventions. They could be who they
wanted to be. The moor and nature in general
was their passion.

21 a. made   b. locked   c. comforting   d. given
e. left   f. standing   g. seen   h. allowed
22 a. bored   b. terrified   c. worrying
d. shocked
23 a. afraid   b. fond   c. worried   f. curious
g. kind   h. cruel
24 a. afraid   b. curious   c. fond   d. kind

Test

1 a. 2   b. 1   c. 1   d. 2
2 a. 2   b. 4   c. 1   d. 2   e. 3